"I'm sure you've heard of Gabriel Flanagan, our city's firefighter hero."

Nolie looked. Well over six feet of glowering firefighter glared back at her. Gabriel Flanagan didn't seem to be any more enthusiastic about this than she was.

"We have to set a deadline. Suppose we say one month from today. You can report back to us, and we'll make a final decision about the grant." The director beamed. "I'm sure we'll all be pleased with the results."

The expensive office shimmered in front of her eyes. One month. One month to successfully pair a service dog with a man who looked as if he'd rather do just about anything than come anywhere near her and her program.

* * *

Books by Marta Perry

Love Inspired

*Hometown Heroes
†Caldwell Kin
**The Flanagans

MARTA PERRY

has written everything from Sunday school curriculum to travel articles to magazine stories in twenty years of writing, but she feels she's found her writing home in the stories she writes for Love Inspired.

Marta lives in rural Pennsylvania, but she and her husband spend part of each year at their second home in South Carolina. When she's not writing, she's probably visiting her children and her beautiful grandchildren, traveling or relaxing with a good book.

Marta loves hearing from readers and she'll write back with a signed bookplate or bookmark. Write to her c/o Steeple Hill Books, 233 Broadway, New York, NY 10279, e-mail her at marta@martaperry.com or visit her on the Web at www.martaperry.com.

HERO IN HER HEART

MARTA PERRY

Published by Steeple Hill Books™

STEEPLE HILL BOOKS

Steeple Hill®

ISBN 0-373-87259-3

HERO IN HER HEART

Copyright © 2004 by Martha Johnson

This edition published by arrangement with Steeple Hill Books.

® and TM are trademarks of Steeple Hill Books, used under license. Trademarks indicated with ® are registered in the United States Patent and Trademark Office, the Canadian Trade Marks Office and in other countries.

Visit us at www.steeplehill.com

Printed in U.S.A.

Therefore let us draw near with confidence
to the throne of grace, so that we may receive
mercy and find grace to help in times of need.
—*Hebrews* 4:16

This story is dedicated to my dear brother, William Perry, his wife, Molly, and their loving family, with much love.

Chapter One

Therefore let us draw near with confidence to the throne of grace, so that we may receive mercy and find grace to help in times of need.

Hebrews 4:16

Nolie Lang stared at the elderly philanthropist who'd just offered her her heart's desire with some unexpected conditions attached.

"I'm sorry." She probably sounded like an idiot, but that was how she'd felt since the moment she'd stepped into the plush offices of the Henley Foundation. "What did you say?"

Samuel Henley, beaming all over his rosy, wrinkled face, looked like one of Santa's elves. Unfortunately, he didn't sound like one. "I said we have the perfect test case to determine if your project is worth our foundation's funding." He gestured toward one of the two men sitting opposite her. "I'm sure you've heard of Gabriel Flanagan, our city's firefighter hero."

Nolie looked. Well over six feet of glowering firefighter glared back at her. Gabriel Flanagan didn't seem to be any more enthusiastic about this than she was.

"Yes, of course I have." Flanagan's picture had been in all the newspapers a month or two ago, when he'd been injured while rescuing several people from a burning warehouse. "But I didn't realize Mr. Flanagan's injuries required the services of a seizure dog."

She couldn't miss Flanagan's reaction to that comment, even though she was usually better at reading animals than people. Without saying a word, he rejected what she'd said completely.

He resembled nothing so much as a dog with its hackles raised. Flanagan was an Irish name, but Gabriel wasn't remotely like an Irish setter. He was more of a bull mastiff—big, guarded, wary and vaguely threatening.

The silence was stretching too long. She, Henley and the man who'd been introduced as Suffolk's fire chief all seemed to wait for a response from Flanagan. It didn't come.

The fire chief planted beefy hands on equally beefy knees and leaned forward. "Gabe got a head injury in the accident." He slid a sideways glance toward the man. "We're sure he'll recover and be back on the job in no time, but he has had a couple of—" He hesitated, searching for the word. "—episodes."

"Seizures." Flanagan's voice was a ferocious bass rumble, like a threatening growl. "Call it what it is. I had three seizures."

Seizures weren't that unusual after a head injury. "When was the most recent one?" She ventured the question and was rewarded with a flash of barely controlled fury in eyes so deep a blue that they were almost black.

"Two weeks ago." He spat the words out. "That doesn't mean anything. I'm getting better all the time. I don't need some kind of a guide dog to help me."

"Seizure alert dog. Or service dog." She made the correction automatically and then wished she hadn't. Flanagan looked as if it would give him great pleasure to rip her head off.

She couldn't really blame the man. He was obviously in complete denial, which hardly made him a good candidate to convince the Henley Foundation that they should sink a ton of money into saving her service-animal program.

She planted her feet more firmly in plush carpeting that seemed to reach to her ankles. The navy blazer and white shirt that had seemed appropriate when she'd left the farm now felt like rummage-sale leftovers. She inhaled. The office even smelled like money.

I don't belong here, Father, but you know I'll do whatever it takes to help Your little ones.

You can't. Aunt Mariah's voice had rarely echoed in her head in recent years, and now was certainly not a good time for it to start. *You're worthless. Always were, always will be.*

She'd found her own way of dealing with that bitter voice over the years. *I am a child of God, valuable in His sight.*

The words gave her the assurance to face anyone, including eccentric millionaires and angry firefighters.

She cleared her throat. "If Mr. Flanagan is opposed to this, perhaps we could find another client to prove the worth of my program to the foundation."

Henley's rosy face crumpled, as if he were a toddler whose promised ice cream cone had been snatched away.

"Nonsense." The chief's voice boomed. "Of course Flanagan wants to do this. He can't wait to get started." He shot Gabe a look that demanded agreement.

Obviously Chief Donovan had no intention of offending the man whose generosity to the city of Suffolk, Pennsylvania, was legendary. Well, she didn't want to offend Henley, either. She wanted him to come forth with the grant for Nolie's Ark that would give many more people service dogs to make their lives easier.

She suppressed a flicker of panic. With the rising taxes on farmland, how much longer could she keep going if the foundation didn't help?

"Yes." Flanagan ground out the word. If his square jaw got any tighter, it might break. "I'm willing to cooperate."

They were the appropriate words, but every line of his tense body said cooperation was out of the question.

Nolie's heart sank. She couldn't hope to convince the foundation that her program worked if her test case were determined to reject everything she had to offer.

"That's good." She tried to pretend she believed him. She focused on Henley across the barricade of the desk. He was the one she had to convince, not Flanagan. "But as you know, my work is primarily with children. I'm not sure that Mr. Flanagan is the best candidate."

"You do work with adults, too." Henley put a manicured hand on the navy folder in which she'd submitted her proposal. The cheap folder looked out of place on the expanse of polished mahogany. "You mentioned that in your application."

She was going to have some fierce words for Claire. Her best friend had been supremely confident that convincing Henley she deserved the grant would be a snap. Maybe it would be, for someone as polished and savvy as Claire.

Unfortunately plain old country girl Nolie Lang was the one who had to do the convincing.

"Pairing a seizure dog with a client depends on the rapport between client and animal. That's easier to achieve with a young client."

Was she beginning to sound desperate? That was how she felt, but desperation probably wasn't the best feeling to convey if she expected the man to fund her work.

"Gabriel Flanagan is the foundation's choice."

She caught the glimpse of steel in Henley's rosy face. The implication was clear. This would be done his way or not at all.

For a moment she didn't seem to see the elegant office with its wide windows looking out on the centuries-old city square. Instead she saw her farm, her animals and the people she could help with this money. Especially the children she could help.

She forced a smile. "If that's how you feel about it, I'd be happy to work with Mr. Flanagan."

She couldn't help but glance in the firefighter's direction. He glared back at her, as if furious that she'd agreed.

Her own anger sparked. If Flanagan didn't want to do this, he was the one who should speak up.

"Excellent," Henley said, rubbing his palms together in pleasure. "I'm delighted you both see it my way."

As if either of them had a choice in the matter. Well, she'd certainly try this, but she had a bad feeling about what Flanagan was bringing to the situation.

"Now tell me," Henley went on. "How do you usually begin work?"

Maybe it would be better not to let her gaze stray toward Gabe Flanagan. "Ordinarily I visit the client's home first, but—"

"Good." Chief Donovan planted his hands on the arms of his chair, as if ready to have this meeting over. "Gabe needs a ride, so you can drive him home now. That way you can meet all of the Flanagans at once."

His tone made it sound as if that should be a real treat for her. Her apprehension grew. She wasn't much good with families, and she didn't suppose the Flanagans would be any different.

"Fine." Henley got to his feet, seeming to take her agreement for granted. The rest of them followed suit. Apparently the audience was over. She turned toward the door, not looking forward to the moment when she'd be alone with Gabe Flanagan.

"One last thing," Henley said.

She swung back around, apprehension a hard ball in her stomach.

A ray of afternoon sunlight made Henley's white hair glisten. ''We have to set a deadline, of course. Suppose we say one month from today. You can report back to us, and we'll make a final decision about the grant.'' He beamed. ''I'm sure we'll all be pleased with the results.''

The expensive office shimmered in front of her eyes. One month. One month to successfully pair a service dog with a man who looked as if he'd rather do just about anything than come anywhere near her and her program.

She squared her shoulders, reaching deep for confidence. Her work deserved the support of the Henley grant. She had to believe that if she were to make a difference.

Like it or not, Gabe Flanagan was essential to her success. That meant she had to make the man cooperate, whether he wanted to or not.

Gabe followed the Lang woman out into the tiled hallway, feeling as if he'd been kicked in the gut. He'd expected this little soirée to be bad. He just hadn't expected it to be that bad.

Anger and resentment roiled through him. This wasn't fair. The chief had no right to subject him to this humiliation.

Nolie Lang punched the elevator button. He stood behind her, seething. He would not favor his bad leg when he moved. He could control the limp. He couldn't control the seizures.

A chill went down his spine. What if he had one

right here, right now, falling down in front of her on the polished tile floor?

No. That wasn't going to happen. He'd had his last seizure, he was sure of it.

He shook his head, feeling like a bull shaking off a swarm of angry bees. People had been shooting darts into his hide since the accident. First it was the doctor, saying he couldn't predict if or when the lesion on his brain would heal. Then his mother, fussing over him endlessly and insisting he move back home to recuperate.

A fat lot of good that had done. He'd given up trying to feel human again while watching his father and brothers kid him about taking a vacation from work as they tried to hide the fear in their eyes that he'd never be back to normal.

The elevator came. Nolie Lang stepped in, and he followed her. At least she was quiet. He'd expected her to be on him the moment they left the office, trying to convince him that this program of hers would work.

Apparently she'd nearly persuaded Samuel Henley. So Henley had leaned on the chief, and the chief had leaned on him. The pecking order at work…and he was caught in it. Either he volunteered for the Lang woman's project or he wouldn't be returning to active duty any time soon.

Nolie Lang didn't look like a very formidable barrier. She was almost plain, with her tanned face free of makeup and her pale blond hair held back with a tie at the nape of her neck. *Repressed,* maybe that was the word. The only time he'd seen passion in those light blue eyes had been when she'd talked about her work.

Her work. She didn't want Gabe Flanagan. She wanted a guinea pig on which to try out her theories.

Well, it wasn't going to be him. He almost said so, but the elevator reached the garage level, and the few minutes it took to evade several people getting on while they got off was long enough to make him think before he spoke.

He wanted out of this business, but he couldn't get out. So he had to convince the woman to let him off the hook. Nolie Lang was just another obstacle to his getting back to the work he was born to do. He'd go through her if he had to, but first he'd try getting her to cooperate with him.

Their feet echoed on the concrete floor of the parking level. She glanced at him.

"Is your leg bothering you?"

A flame of anger went through him that he'd let his guard slip, made hotter that she'd noticed.

"No." That came out almost like a snarl, which was not the way to gain the woman's cooperation. "It's healing."

"That's good." She walked briskly toward a dusty station wagon, apparently not concerned enough about his leg to slow down. Or maybe she took him at his word that he was all right.

"Look." His voice halted her as she unlocked the wagon, her square, competent hand freezing on the handle. "Maybe we ought to talk. We both know Henley's idea is a bad one."

She surveyed him, her eyes expressionless. "I generally find that's not a good thing to say to the man with the money."

He hunched his shoulders. "That's what the chief

thinks, too. But that doesn't mean this is going to work.''

''Maybe.'' She swung the passenger door open and held it for him.

Resentment bubbled again as he swung himself inside. He didn't like depending on other people to haul him around. The first thing that had happened after he'd had a seizure was the doctor pulling his driver's license.

She rounded the car and got in. He swallowed the urge to rant at her. Think, don't react, he commanded himself.

''What's this for?'' He tapped the mesh screen behind the front seat as she turned the ignition.

''Keeps the dogs from jumping in front.''

''I thought your animals were well-trained enough to help people. Surely they don't misbehave in the car.''

If the jab bothered her, she didn't show it. She just backed out and started down the winding concrete ramp.

''Sometimes I pick up strays.'' She slowed as they reached the garage exit. ''Which way?''

''Go right.'' Okay, maybe annoying her wasn't the best way of getting her on his side. ''Look, you said it yourself. I'm not a good candidate for this project.''

Her cool profile didn't tell him a thing about what she was feeling. ''I only said that if you weren't interested, this probably wouldn't work well.''

''I'm not interested.'' He fought the longing to shout the words at her. ''I'm only doing this because the chief insisted, and he's not a man you can argue with.''

He was also the man who held the power to decide whether Gabe went back on active duty or had to settle for a desk job. Or, worse, a disability retirement.

No. The denial burned in his brain.

"It seems to me we're both stuck." She brushed a strand of pale blond hair behind her ear. "You have to do what your chief says. I have to do what Henley says if I want to get my grant."

"You could talk to him again. Tell him someone else would work out better."

Her hands moved restlessly on the wheel, stroking it as if it were a pet. "He wants you."

"Because of the publicity." Pictures of him on the front page of the local paper, flanked by pictures of the two firefighters who'd died that day.

"I suppose even philanthropists want positive publicity. You're a hero."

The word dropped on him like acid. "Believe me, nothing is staler than yesterday's hero."

"Obviously, Samuel Henley doesn't think so." She slanted a sideways glance at him. "Why does it matter so much to you?"

The attack went under his guard, and for a moment he couldn't speak.

"It doesn't," he said when he thought he could control his voice. "I'm just saying that the whole idea is futile. As I understand it, you need someone who can prove this seizure dog thing of yours works."

"I already know it works." There was that passion again, flaring in her eyes as she shot a look at him.

"Okay, bad choice of words. You need someone to show the foundation the value of it." He leaned forward. "Turn right at the next corner."

She took the turn onto Elm Street. Thanks to Dutch elm disease, the street was now lined with maples, but no one had suggested changing the name. The May sunshine had brought into full bloom the magnolia tree his mother had planted in the front yard.

"This one." He nodded toward the sprawling brick two-story his grandfather had built for his expanding family.

The current generation filled it up, too. He tensed at the sight of the cars in the curving driveway. It looked as if the whole family was here.

She stopped the car and turned to look at him, apparently knowing he had more to say on the subject.

"I'm not the right person to prove the worth of your program." He leaned toward her, intent on convincing her he was right about this. "And it's not because I'm stubborn or uncooperative."

A smile flickered on her face, the first one he'd seen. It showed him an unexpected pair of dimples in her cheeks that made her seem both younger and more vulnerable. "It's not?"

"No." He had to be sure she understood this. "This seizure-alert thing only works if the person actually has seizures, right?"

"Of course." Her eyes were wary.

"Then I'm no good to you. Because I'm not going to have any more seizures."

She looked at him steadily for a long moment, and he didn't have the slightest idea if she bought it. Then she lifted a level eyebrow.

"Will your doctor confirm that?"

His fists clenched. "Take my word for it. I won't be a help to you. So the sooner you convince Henley this isn't going to work, the sooner we can both get on with our lives.''

It was a nice speech. Unfortunately Nolie Lang looked at him as if she didn't believe a word of it.

The approach of a woman who was probably Gabe's mother prevented Nolie from replying. Good timing, because almost anything she said would have led to an explosion on Gabe's part.

Did Gabe have any idea how deeply into denial he was? Probably not, or he'd show some sign that he didn't quite believe his own words.

What if he's right? The insidious question slipped into her mind as she got out of the car. If Gabe's injury had healed, she'd be in the unique position of trying to demonstrate her techniques on someone who would never need them. And Samuel Henley would have put a condition on his grant that she could never fulfill.

Head swimming, she pasted a smile on her face and turned to the woman who'd come to greet them.

"Gabe." Mrs. Flanagan had a quick smile and a pat on the cheek for her son. The unconscious lovingness of the gesture grabbed Nolie's heart.

The woman held out her hand. "You must be Ms. Lang. I'm Siobhan Flanagan. Welcome to our home."

Nolie looked into eyes that were as deeply blue as Gabe's, but far less guarded. A few lines on her fair skin spoke of life experience, but only a strand or two of gray accented her black hair. Again, like her son's.

"Thank you. It's a pleasure to meet you."

Nolie shook hands, wondering a little. Gabe hadn't called his mother, but she'd obviously known to expect them. That must mean the fire chief had called her, indicating a close relationship between them. She filed that fact away for later consideration.

"You come right on in." Mrs. Flanagan linked her arm with Nolie's. "We're all eager to get to know you."

All? Nolie took note of the cars lining the drive. "It looks as if you're having a party. I can come another time."

That actually brought a short bark of laughter from Gabe, following them up the walk. "No party. Just the usual crush of Flanagans."

Mrs. Flanagan had a firm grip on her arm. Short of yanking herself free, she seemed to be stuck.

Gabe opened the front door, and a wave of sound hit her, taking her breath away. Apparently all the Flanagans were talking at once.

Gabe's mother seemed to sniff the air. "Goodness, my stew." She patted Nolie's arm. "You'll stay for supper with us. Don't you run away until we have a chance to talk."

She scurried off. She couldn't know just how much Nolie wanted to run away.

Don't be ridiculous. They can't hurt you. She had to lecture herself on the subject of families now and then. Every family wasn't like hers, after all.

And if she could gain the family's cooperation, her work with Gabe might be considerably easier. So she'd do this.

People seemed to swirl through the huge living room and dining room that stretched the entire width of the house. She had a quick impression of comfortably overstuffed furniture and walls crowded with family photos—dozens of family photos.

Gabe was still at her side, and she could feel the solid strength of him through the brush of his arm against hers. She sought for something to say. "You have a big family."

"You might say that. My parents have five kids, although sometimes it seems like more."

"And you all live at home?"

Gabe's eyes flickered with a touch of regret. "I have my own place. I moved home after the accident."

She added that fact to her mental calculations of the dog who would be best for Gabe, always assuming he stayed with the program long enough to get a dog.

"I guess that seems odd, but my folks are old-fashioned." He sounded slightly defensive. "They want their kids to live at home until they're married."

"Or longer." The speaker must be one of Gabe's brothers, since he had the trademark deep blue eyes and black hair. Probably in his mid twenties, he had an engaging liveliness to his face, and he carried a wiggling toddler under one arm. "I thought we'd never get Mary Kate out of the house." He held out his hand to Nolie. "I'm Ryan."

"The baby." A red-haired woman arrived at his elbow. "I'm Mary Kate." She started to shake hands with Nolie, then abruptly turned away to grab the toddler Ryan was dangling. "How many times have we told you not to hold Davy upside down? You want him to throw up on you? Come help me put a leaf in the table."

They left before Nolie had a chance to say anything, even assuming she could have thought of something. She glanced at Gabe, to find him watching her with amusement.

"They're a bit much, I grant you. Mary Kate's the oldest, and the two red-haired hooligans are hers." He nodded toward a boy and girl chasing each other. "I'm next, then Seth, then Theresa, then Ryan. The little guy Ryan was holding is Seth's son, Davy. Don't worry about remembering their names."

Because she wouldn't be around long enough for it to matter?

"I don't want to impose." What she wanted was to get out of this crowd and back to her quiet house. Alone. "I just needed to get a sense of what your home life was like so that I can choose an appropriate animal."

"My mother would consider it an insult if you left now."

He nodded to Siobhan, who was clinking a spoon on a glass. The signal sent her family scurrying to the dining-room table—a long walnut oval covered by a lace tablecloth.

She could guess that Gabe's opinion didn't match his mother's. Still, she needed all the help she could get with the man. If she didn't win him over—

She stopped that thought before it could take over. She managed a smile and let herself be piloted to a seat.

The man next to her was obviously Gabe's father, and just as obviously the patriarch of the clan. He sat in a massive chair at the head of the table, watching benevolently as his family took their places.

He didn't say anything, just waited as they quieted and clasped hands around the table. Before she quite knew how it had happened, Nolie felt her hands held firmly by Gabe's father on one side and the sister she hadn't been introduced to on the other—Theresa, she thought.

Mr. Flanagan led them in grace, a very faint Irish accent touching the words of the prayer as it rolled out. His Amen was punctuated by the clatter of dishes.

"Getting us all sorted out yet?" Gabe's sister, Theresa, had a quick smile. "My father is Joe, and I'm Terry. I'm afraid we can be overwhelming at first glance."

"And at second," Ryan added from across the table.

"I think I'm getting there." She glanced around, sorting out Mary Kate, her husband and children.

Terry grinned. "Mary Kate, Seth and I got Dad's red hair and freckles, but Seth's darkened when he grew up. Gabe and Ryan look like Mom."

She nodded, wondering whether learning their names was of any use. If Gabe had his way, this could be the first and last time she met the Flanagans.

Seth was the solid, calm one, then. He sat next to the toddler, rescuing the teething biscuit the child dropped. "And Davy's mother?"

Sorrow darkened Terry's lively face. "She died shortly after he was born. Davy lives here with us."

The sorrow touched her. "You must be very close."

"We are that." Gabe's father had obviously heard her comment. "Every single one a firefighter, and proud of it."

She blinked. "You're all firefighters?"

"Well, not Siobhan. And not Mary Kate, now that she has a family. But her husband filled in for her, didn't you, Kenny?"

Mary Kate's husband stopped buttering bread for one of his children to nod, smiling.

"That's amazing." Would that make it easier or harder to enlist their aid with Gabe? She didn't know.

Joe Flanagan shrugged. "It's what we do. What we were born for. Maybe Gabe most of all." He leaned toward her, lowering his voice. "Gabe is strong as a horse. He'll be back on the job in no time. I'm not saying anything against this program of yours, but Gabe doesn't need it."

"I see." That seemed to answer the question of whether she could expect any help from Gabe's family. His father, at least, was just as convinced as Gabe that Nolie was unnecessary.

Her head began to throb from the noise. She glanced at Gabe, wondering how he stood it all.

But Gabe was leaning back in his chair, gesturing with his fork at something one of his brothers had said. His angular face was the most relaxed she'd seen it. His hair, nearly blue-black where the overhead light reflected on it, tumbled onto his forehead a little.

As if he felt her gaze on him, he looked at her. His face was open to her for just an instant, and her heart seemed to turn over. Her breath caught, and the noise around them faded.

Whoa. She'd better be careful. Because if Gabriel Flanagan looked at her that way too many times, she'd could find herself agreeing with just about anything he said.

Chapter Two

By the time supper ended, Gabe was beginning to think he'd never get rid of Nolie Lang. Every member of his family seemed determined to talk to her. He could only hope they were all telling her the same thing he had—that he didn't need her help. The woman should leave convinced she'd have to find another guinea pig for her experiment.

Judging by the way Nolie's gaze kept darting toward the door, she was ready to be free of the Flanagans, too, for the moment, at least. Well, he wanted her to be free of them permanently.

He'd steered clear while Mom had showed her the wall full of fire-department photos and citations above the mantel, not wanting to be the subject of his mother's praises in front of this woman.

But now Ryan joined them, chatting away as if he and Nolie were old friends. Gabe hoped he was reinforcing the family line—Gabe doesn't need your help. Gabe is fine. Gabe will be back on the job in no time.

Ryan seemed to be turning on an inordinate amount of the Flanagan charm. Now, why was his little brother going to so much trouble? It certainly wasn't as if Nolie were his type. Ryan might be initially attracted by the long blond hair, but everything else about Nolie would turn him off.

Plain. That was all he could think. She looked as if she hadn't made the faintest effort—just run in from the barn and tossed on a white shirt and navy blazer. Even his tomboy sister Terry would have done a better job for an important interview.

So what interested Ryan so much? He sauntered closer to find out.

"That's my father and his brothers when they first joined the department."

Ryan had obviously taken over the explanations, while his mother smiled and nodded. Nolie couldn't know it, but the Flanagan kids favored either Mom or Dad in personality as well as looks. Mary Kate, Terry and Ryan were as ebullient as Dad, while he and Seth had his mother's reserve.

Ryan's eyes sparked with mischief as Gabe joined them. "And here's the brand-new citation for our latest hero, Gabriel Flanagan."

Nolie studied the plaque with every indication of interest. Gabe averted his eyes from it and glared at his brother.

"Give it a rest, Ryan."

"Hey, I will when you stop gold-bricking and get back on the job. I don't want to have to uphold the family traditions single-handedly."

"You've got Dad, Seth and Terry to do that."

He could only hope they were also keeping Ryan

in line. The kid had a tendency to take more risks than he needed to at times.

"They're not the current hero." Ryan, of course, knew exactly what buttons to push.

"Knock it off." That came out with enough of a snarl in his voice that even his baby brother knew he meant it.

With another engaging grin for Nolie, Ryan moved away.

"We are proud of you," his mother said softly. "You know that, don't you?"

"Sure, Mom." He dropped a quick kiss on her cheek. "I understand, but Nolie didn't come to hear the whole Flanagan saga."

"Actually it's quite helpful in deciding what kind of dog will work best for you," Nolie said. "I'm finding it all very interesting."

She was probably picturing the publicity she'd get for her program with him as her prized exhibit. Well, he wasn't going to join her dog-and-pony show, not if he could help it.

A clatter of dishes from the kitchen diverted his mother. She murmured an apology and scurried in that direction.

As soon as she'd gone, he squared off with Nolie. "I already told you. I don't need a dog."

Her level brows lifted. "I believe I heard you tell the chief that you'd cooperate."

"What I told—" he began.

"Are you seeing all the family history?" This time the interruption came from a man new to the gathering, and he gritted his teeth before attempting introductions.

"Nolie Lang, this is my cousin, Brendan Flanagan. Come to scrounge some leftovers, no doubt."

Brendan's grin admitted the truth of that barb. "Only partly. I also wanted to meet Ms. Lang."

"Nolie, please." She extended her hand. "Are you another of the Flanagan firefighters?"

Brendan shook his head, probably used to explaining his story.

"I'm the one holdout—the only Flanagan who didn't go into the family business. I'm the minister at Grace Church."

Gabe couldn't miss Nolie's reaction to that. She snatched her hand back as if she'd touched hot metal, and her skin went pale under her tan.

Now what, exactly, was going on with the woman?

"Brendan keeps us in line," Gabe said with deliberate casualness, watching her. "If all the Flanagans aren't sitting in a row on Sunday morning, he wants to know why."

"And I'm also the fire department chaplain, so they can't get away from me at work, either," Brendan added. "Which I guess means I didn't completely reject the family business."

He could tell by the way Brendan studied Nolie's face that he'd noted her intense reaction, too.

"I see." She gave a meaningless smile, and he sensed that only strong control kept her from bolting out the door. She fumbled in her pocket and pulled out a card. "Here's my address," she said, handing it to Gabe. "I'd like to meet at the farm tomorrow, if that's possible for you."

His jaw clenched. "I don't think I can make it."

Their gazes clashed, and he saw a determination in

hers that matched his own. "I think you'd better find a way."

The implication was clear. He'd show up, or she'd sic the chief on him.

"Fine." He ground out the word. "What time?"

"About one o'clock would be good for me."

She waited long enough for his curt nod, and then turned toward the door. "Please thank your parents for me. I really have to leave."

She didn't wait for a response, just bolted toward the exit with barely concealed relief.

Gabe let the door close behind her before he looked at his cousin, eyebrows lifting.

"Okay, let me in on the secret. Exactly what did you do to the woman to send her running?"

Brendan shrugged, his eyes troubled. "I don't know. She seems to have a problem with ministers, doesn't she?"

"Obviously. You don't usually send strange women screaming for the exit."

That didn't bring the smile he expected from Brendan. "I'd like to talk with her further. Maybe when you're working with her, you can mention that I'd enjoy getting to know her better."

"I don't intend to be working with her, remember?"

"So I've heard." Brendan's gaze probed beneath the surface. "You want to talk about that?"

No. He didn't. He didn't want to talk about any of it.

"Thanks anyway, Brendan. Save the pastoral advice for somebody who needs it. I'm fine."

Fine. He certainly didn't want to talk to his cousin

about the fact that he seemed to be going through the motions spiritually these days. Or that God had been silent just when he needed Him most.

And he also didn't intend to discuss his vulnerabilities with Nolie Lang. Determination tensed every muscle. This little encounter hadn't worked out as well as he'd hoped. Even the Flanagan crew hadn't been able to convince her he didn't need her services.

But the next day they'd be alone together, without his loving, interfering family around. They'd have it out.

He wasn't going to be Nolie's test case. Tomorrow he'd make sure she accepted that fact.

Gabe hadn't shown up. One o'clock had come and gone, and he hadn't even called. Nolie couldn't say she was surprised.

She tried to concentrate on getting Danny Trent and his wheelchair through the obstacle course she'd set up in the renovated garage that was now her training center. She'd left the big doors open, and May sunshine warmed the concrete floor.

One might expect that the eight-year-old, with his multiple birth defects and his feuding parents, would be tough to work with, but he wasn't. Danny's indomitable spirit shone through no matter what struggle he faced.

At the moment he was adjusting to training with Lady, the German shepherd she'd chosen for him. Both took to their challenges eagerly, and her heart warmed with the joy of a successful pairing.

"Great job, Danny."

Danny rewarded her with the smile that seemed too big for his small face. "Thanks."

"Now tell Lady what a good girl she is and give her a treat."

She watched as he struggled to make his hand co-operate in giving Lady the doggie nugget. It was hard not to jump in and help when he had difficulty, but Danny could do this himself. Every little triumph gave him energy for the next challenge.

The boy beamed when he succeeded. Lady licked his cheek, making him giggle.

"Can we do it again, Nolie? Please?"

"Sure, give it another try."

He'd do it faster this time, with more confidence. Gabe ought to see this. Maybe Danny's efforts would help him to understand what her program was all about.

She couldn't say she'd done a very good job of dealing with the man. She'd like to blame it on being knocked off balance by the unexpected condition Henley had put on her grant, but that wasn't all that had gone wrong.

She'd found Flanagan himself intimidating, although she'd certainly never let him know it. His fierce anger at what had happened to him was almost palpable. He couldn't admit that. He was in complete denial about the entire situation.

As for that visit to his house—well, she'd been grateful to escape back to the solitude of her own little world. The Flanagan brood was a little overwhelming.

Unfortunately, *escape* was the right word. She'd basically run like a deer after that unexpected encounter with Gabe's cousin. The minister.

The very word left a sour taste in her mouth. That was what Brother Joshua had called himself, although certainly no divinity school had ever claimed him. And she doubted that God had given any sort of blessing to the man.

None of that had mattered to the great-aunt who'd reluctantly taken her in after everyone else had abandoned her. To put it in the most charitable light, Aunt Mariah hadn't known what to do with a thrown-away eight-year-old. So she'd turned to the leader of her bizarre sect for child-rearing advice.

I know I should get over this, Father. My relationship with You transcends anything in my past. It does. But every time I come into contact with organized religion, all those dark memories come back.

Well, she didn't have to have anything more to do with Gabe's cousin. And it looked as if she might not be able to have anything more to do with Gabe, either.

What were her options? She could confront him again. Or go to the fire chief for help. Or even contact the foundation, although she certainly didn't want to admit failure to Samuel Henley at the first hurdle.

"We did it!" Danny crowed. "We did perfect, No-lie."

"You sure did, honey." She managed to hug him and ruffle the dog's fur at the same time. "You'll be ready for graduation before you know it."

His face clouded. "I don't want to—not if I have to go away from you."

"Hey, it's okay." Her heart clenched. "I'll always be your friend, you know that."

But they would part. That was the nature of her work. She bonded with a child or an animal, worked intensely with them for months, and then saw them leave. That was success—they didn't need her anymore.

She planted a kiss on Danny's cheek. "Your mom's here to pick you up. I'll see you next time."

She straightened, trying to keep the smile on her face. Danny's mother wasn't the only one here. Gabe lounged in the doorway, watching her.

Tension zinged along her nerves. She'd rather work with a dozen Dannys than one large, angry male, but she didn't have a choice.

She waved goodbye to the child and tried to put a little steel in her spine as she walked toward Gabe, Lady trotting at her heels. She wouldn't let the man intimidate her. She would show him the work she did here so convincingly that he'd have to admit its value.

And make him admit he needed it? Probably not, but she had to try.

"Good afternoon." She wouldn't say anything about his tardiness. Let him bring it up if he wanted.

He gave a curt nod. The jeans and white knit shirt he wore today contrasted with the dress shirt and slacks he'd had on at the foundation the day before. His shoulders seemed even broader, his frown more intimidating.

She wiped her palms on her own faded jeans. He was not going to succeed in cowing her.

"That's a cute kid." When he finally spoke, it was about Danny.

"Yes, he is." Her gaze softened as she watched the boy's mother settle him into her van and fold his wheelchair with the ease of long practice.

"What's wrong with him?"

Lady nuzzled Gabe's leg, curious about the stranger, and he scratched her ears absently.

Good. At least he related to a dog without tension or fear. "Danny has multiple birth defects. He may always have to depend on the chair, but he and Lady are going to be a good team."

He glanced down at Lady. "Why didn't the dog go home with him?"

"They have a lot of training to do with me before that happens. But Danny's a hard worker. He'll make it." *What about you, Gabe? Will you give me a chance to help you?*

"Meaning you think I'm not." He shot the words at her.

She couldn't argue with everything he said, or they'd never get anything done. "I guess we'll see, won't we?"

She gestured around the expanse of concrete, with its hurdles, barricades, ramps and stairs. "This is our training area. Clients and animals learn to work together here."

"Don't you mean dogs?"

At least something interested him. "Mostly dogs, but not always. I've trained monkeys to help people who have limited use of their hands. Different animals meet different needs." She stroked Lady. "Lady will help Danny learn to maneuver in his chair, keep him safe and protect him if he falls."

"That's a big job for an animal." He was still frowning, but at least he wasn't walking away.

"Lady can handle it. She loves to work. I'm hoping that eventually she'll be able to alert him." She hesitated, and then deliberately added, "Danny has a seizure disorder, too. Maybe you ought to talk with him about it.''

''No.'' The word snapped out at her, sharp as a slap.

''It could help both of you.''

His hands clenched, as if he didn't know what to do with his stress. ''Look, I did tell the chief I'd cooperate, so I'm here. But don't try putting me in a box with your other patients. I won't fit.''

Patience, Nolie, patience.

''So where does the cooperating part come in?''

He didn't smile, but some of the tension went out of his face. ''Like I said, I'm here. I'm ready to be convinced that what you do is legitimate.''

He wasn't ready to be convinced of anything at all, but at least he'd come. Maybe she could still salvage this project once he saw what she actually did here.

''Let's see the rest of the operation,'' Nolie said. She led the way outside, blinking as she stepped into the bright May sunshine.

Gabe's sister, Terry, sat in a dusty van pulled up under the oak tree next to the drive. She waved in their direction, but didn't get out.

''Your sister's welcome to come look around.''

He shook his head. ''She's prepping for some paramedic test she has coming up. I told her she could use the time for studying.''

He clearly hated depending on other people to take him places. Maybe he also resented the fact that other people's careers moved on while his stagnated.

''There's my house.'' She gestured toward the white frame building with its black shutters, a typical Pennsylvania farmhouse nestled into the lush green

fields that had drawn Pennsylvania Dutch farmers to
the area a century earlier. "And the outbuildings."

Gabe glanced at the cottage that was tucked into the
grove of hemlocks behind the main house. "Space for
visiting relatives?"

"Not exactly." Gabe, with his huge, supportive
clan, couldn't possibly imagine the isolation of having
no one. "I fixed up the guest cottage for clients to use
during the final phase of training."

He sent her a wary look. "Final phase? That sounds
ominous."

"In the early stages of training, I work with the
client and the service animal several times a week. The
last two weeks are intensive training, and the client
lives in the cottage with the animal."

Somehow she thought Gabe would balk at that,
even if he agreed to the rest of the program. Well,
she'd handle that when the time came. The important
thing now was simply to gain his agreement.

"How long does all this take?"

"Usually a couple of months, at least. But since Mr.
Henley put a month limit on us, we'll have to accelerate the process for you."

She waited for him to reiterate that he didn't need
the program, but he merely nodded toward the white-
rail-fenced paddock as they approached it. "More
trained animals, or just color?"

She leaned on the top rail, clicking her fingers. The
gray donkey ambled over to have his floppy ears
scratched. "This is Toby. The humane society took
him from an abusive owner and asked me to give him
a home. As you say, he adds a little color. The children
like him, and he's certified as a therapeutic pet."

Gabe reached across the railing to rub Toby's muzzle. Toby stared back with mournful brown eyes. "A therapeutic pet," he repeated.

"Sorry." She smiled. "You don't know the lingo yet. A therapeutic pet is an animal that's trained to go into places like nursing homes to relate to the patients."

"You take a donkey into a nursing home?" He clearly didn't believe that was possible.

"Hey, he's a big hit, especially with the ladies."

Gabe stared at the next animal that wandered up to the fence for her share of attention. "What on earth is that?"

Nolie patted Dixie. "Dixie's a miniature horse. Haven't you ever seen one before?"

He shook his head, his gaze moving between Dixie and the German shepherd. They were about the same size. "Just part of the menagerie?"

"Dixie's training as a service animal. She's going to be a guide animal for a client who is blind."

"You've got to be kidding."

At least she'd captured his interest, even if the gaze he turned on her continued to be disbelieving.

"Miniature horses are good at that. They're intelligent, loyal and they have a longer working lifespan than a dog. It's devastating to a blind person to lose a service dog."

His shoulders moved, as if he didn't want to think about that. "I guess it would be. I can't imagine depending on an animal that way."

"That's what we're all about here. Animals and clients learn to depend on each other."

She couldn't miss his response to that. He didn't

say a word, but his whole body rejected it. Gabe clearly didn't plan to depend on anyone or anything.

"Shall we get on with the grand tour?" His voice had cooled even more.

"All that's left is the barn." Lady pressed against her leg, whining a little. "Go on, girl. You've earned a play time." Lady ducked under the rail, and danced toward the donkey.

Nolie moved quickly toward the open doors of the red barn. She ought to press the subject that burned in her mind, but she wasn't sure how to go about it.

Should she just introduce him to the dog she'd chosen for him? Assume he intended to go through with the program and risk his walking away?

Gabe paused as she waded through a cluster of hens fighting over a kernel of corn. His eyebrow quirked. "Guide chickens?"

"I keep them for the eggs." Was he laughing at her? Probably. Well, she didn't care what he thought of her, as long as he didn't keep her from getting her grant.

She stepped into the barn, inhaling its mingled scents of animals, straw and hay. Sunlight, filtering through a few gaps in the siding she'd have to fix before next winter, set dust motes dancing.

Peace. That was what she always felt here. It was more peaceful to her than any church could possibly be. It had been her sanctuary more than once, both in the sense of a place to worship and also of a place to hide.

"Looks as if no one is in residence." Gabe's voice, echoing closer behind her than she'd thought, seemed to make the dust motes shimmer.

"There's someone here." She clicked her fingers, and the yellow Lab rose from the mound of straw that was his favorite napping spot. "You missed him because he's the same color as his bed."

Max came toward them with the natural dignity that was the first thing she'd noticed about the dog when she'd seen him in the shelter. She stroked the warm, golden fur.

"This is Max. He's the dog I've picked out for you."

Gabe's tension level shot up so high that she could feel it prick her skin through the inches that separated them. Max's ears went up, and he moved protectively closer to Nolie's side.

"I've already told you—"

"You've told me you don't need a dog. But obviously your chief thinks you do."

"He doesn't think any such thing. He's just trying to stay on the good side of the Henley Foundation."

"Either way, he said you'd cooperate. *You* said you'd cooperate." She couldn't let him off the hook. The future of her program depended on him.

"You'd be wasting your time with me. Spend it on someone like Danny."

"Your cooperation means the money that will let me help a lot of Dannys." It could mean the survival of the program, but she didn't think she wanted to trust him with that information.

His harassed look said he didn't know how to respond to that. "All you have to do is go to Henley and tell him I'm not a good candidate for your program. You'll get us both out."

"I've already tried that." She was ashamed to admit it. "I saw Henley again this morning."

"What did he say?" He looked like a man who saw his last hope disappearing.

"That I should prove I could work with a difficult case. Like you."

She held her breath. She'd laid it all on the line with Gabe. If he walked away—

For a long moment he stared at her, his eyes bleak. "So we're both stuck." He bit off the words.

Relief flooded through her, but she didn't dare let him see it. "Yes, I guess we are."

A tiny muscle twitched in his jaw. "All right." He spat out the words. "It's going to be a disaster. But I'll try."

Chapter Three

Gabe couldn't believe he was agreeing to this crazy idea. He also couldn't believe he was responding to the happiness he saw shimmering in Nolie's blue eyes. Or that he wanted to go on seeing it there.

He found himself leaning toward her, as if compelled to be closer. She smelled like soap and sunshine. "Nolie—"

"Am I interrupting something?" The clear, high voice from the barn entrance brought him abruptly to his senses.

A good thing.

"Claire. What are you doing here today?" Nolie's voice had warmed in a way he hadn't heard before. Apparently she only used her coolest tones on him.

The woman who strolled slowly toward them was Nolie's opposite in every conceivable way. Hair a rich, deep auburn, mahogany-colored eyes that were expertly made up, clothes she probably thought of as country that were a far cry from Nolie's shabby jeans and T-shirt.

She held out a perfectly manicured hand to him. "I'm Claire Delany. And you are?"

"This is one of my clients," Nolie said quickly.

He thought her cheeks were slightly pinker than they'd been earlier. Because she'd recognized that insane moment when he'd leaned toward her? He hoped not.

"Does this client have a name?"

"Gabriel Flanagan." He could speak for himself. As for whatever that moment had been—well, not attraction. Definitely not.

He shifted his gaze to the dog, finding it easier to look at Max than to meet Nolie's cornflower gaze. "I'd better be on my way."

"I thought we'd spend some time working with Max."

"Your friend is here." And besides, he didn't want to. He wanted to be alone to figure out how he was going to handle this situation.

"Claire will wait." She shot a look at her friend, who nodded.

A relationship between two such different women had to be an unusual one. He pushed the thought aside. He didn't need to know anything about Nolie beyond the obstacle she represented.

"Tomorrow will do as well, won't it? My sister needs to get back."

Nolie nodded reluctantly, probably fearing that if he once got away from her, he wouldn't be back. "All right, tomorrow. Is two o'clock all right?"

"Two it is." He was already moving toward the

door. He'd agree to just about anything right now that would get him out of there. "I'll see you tomorrow."

When he saw Nolie tomorrow, he'd have figured out how to turn this into a stepping stone. Nolie thought they were stuck with each other, and maybe that was true. But if he had to do this, there had to be a way he could use the situation to get himself on active duty again, the sooner the better.

It took a half hour to drive home, and by the time they arrived, the pep talk Terry seemed compelled to give was wearing thin. She meant well, they all did, but nobody seemed to understand that he had to deal with this situation in his own way.

Seth and Ryan were playing one-on-one in the driveway, so Terry stopped at the curb.

"Thanks, baby."

"Ryan's the baby," Terry snapped back automatically.

He grinned, a bit of his good humor restored. "I'll tell him you said so." He started toward his brothers.

"You're not going to play ball, are you?" Terry asked, a hint of worry in her voice.

Ignoring the question, he kept on going. His family alternated between treating him as if nothing had happened and acting as if he were an invalid.

Ryan missed the ball, and he grabbed it.

"How about taking on some real competition?"

He read identical hesitation in both pairs of eyes.

"Are you sure that's a good idea?" Seth said. "I thought you weren't supposed to get stressed."

"You think beating you is stressful? Think again." He dribbled the ball. "Or are you afraid I'm going to fall down on the driveway in a fit?"

"Of course not." Ryan made an unsuccessful effort to steal the ball.

He dribbled past him and shot. The ball rolled around the rim and bounced out. "I'm out of practice."

"You'd better take it easy on that leg, or Mom will be out here yelling at all of us." Seth grabbed the ball. "How did it go today?"

He shrugged. "The net is closing. She claims she tried to get the foundation let her use someone else, but Henley wouldn't."

"The chief won't back down, either. If Dad couldn't budge him, no one will."

"I don't see a way out." He'd snatch it like a loose ball if he did, agreement or not.

"Look, it won't be so bad." Seth was determined to look on the bright side, but that was Seth, everyone's friend. "Even if you don't need the dog, it won't hurt to play along. You can use the time to get your leg strong again, so you can get back on duty."

Ryan popped the ball out of Seth's hands. "Bad advice. Good old reliable Seth, always playing it safe."

Seth flushed. "That's a lot better than taking stupid risks."

He glanced from one to the other. Did that mean Ryan had been skirting the edge again at work? A firefighter couldn't be paralyzed by danger, but he shouldn't flirt with it, either.

"What have you been up to, Ryan? I keep hearing talk that you're taking a few too many chances these days."

Ryan shrugged, giving him a cocky look that said

he thought he was indestructible. "Maybe I'm trying to live up to my brother, the hero."

The flip words drove like a knife into his soul. "I'm not a hero." If he really were a hero, he'd have found a way to save the men who'd died beside him. "Don't you try to be one. We don't need any funerals in the family."

"Hey, lighten up. I didn't mean anything. I just think you ought to risk turning on the famous Flanagan charm, that's all." Ryan grinned. "Believe me, a plain Jane like that woman would eat it right up. And a few words from her might sway the chief's opinion about when you can get back on the line."

Ryan might actually have a point, although he wouldn't tell him so. Only there were a couple of problems with his scenario.

One was that he was no Ryan, able to turn on the Flanagan charm at a moment's notice.

And the other was that Nolie Lang wasn't plain. Somehow his image of her had changed over the afternoon. In her own setting, Nolie had metamorphosed. He saw again her tenderness as she worked with the child. Pictured the passion in her eyes when she defended her work.

No, Nolie was definitely not plain. But she was definitely trouble.

Nolie spotted the car pull into her lane the next afternoon as she finished her session with Danny. At least Gabe had come. And on time, so she could get on with her goal for the day.

Two goals, she amended. The first was to get him

to bond with his dog—a professional goal, one she understood how to approach.

However, she also had a personal goal, and that was trickier. She had to stop herself from responding to his sheer animal magnetism.

Claire, of course, had picked up on that instantly the day before. Given how their friendship had begun, Claire could honestly say she knew more about Nolie than anyone, and she'd seen that betraying flush. Claire had insisted that Gabe felt something, too, claiming she could always tell.

Well, certainly Claire dated more than she did, but that didn't make her an authority on someone like Gabe Flanagan. A lot of emotions welled up when an active, driven man like Gabe had to confront a life-changing injury. That didn't mean any of those emotions had to do with attraction.

She hadn't felt anything, and neither had he. That was what she told Claire, and what she kept telling herself. Unfortunately Claire hadn't believed it.

And as for her—well, if she believed herself, why then was she wearing a knit sweater with her jeans instead of her usual T-shirt? And why had she bothered touching up her lips with lip gloss and letting her hair swing loose on her shoulders?

Claire's acid comments about her everyday attire came back to her, making her smile.

If you won't dress a little better for Flanagan, then at least have pity on those poor chickens. It's a wonder they'll lay a single egg, having to look at you in that ragged T-shirt every day.

Well, she hoped the chickens were happy. When

Claire called later for a report on the day, she could at least say she'd taken her fashion advice.

"Nolie?" Danny tugged on her arm. "Do you think I could meet him?"

"I don't see why not." She waved at Danny's mother, who waited by her van, then wheeled him toward Gabe.

He leaned against the car door, apparently talking to his sister, but he straightened at their approach.

Nothing. You feel nothing, remember?

"Hi. I have someone here who wants to meet you."

Gabe's eyes seemed to darken, and she remembered too late his reaction when she'd suggested he talk to Danny about his seizure disorder.

"Danny, this is Gabriel Flanagan."

"Hi, Danny. It's nice to meet you." Whatever he felt, he masked it as he held out his hand.

It was a long moment until Danny got his muscles to cooperate so that he could extend his hand. To his credit, Gabe didn't show by the smallest flicker that he noticed that. Gabe made some comment about Lady, and they talked dogs as she bent to the car window to greet Terry.

Gabe's sister was on the cell phone, but she smiled and waved.

By the time Nolie had straightened, Danny's mother was wheeling the boy away. She could tell by the boy's beaming face that it had gone well.

Terry leaned across the front seat to get Gabe's attention. "I'm sorry, but I've been called in to work. I'll try and reach Mom to pick you up."

"Mom's going out this afternoon." Gabe's mouth tightened in annoyance, she suspected, that he had to depend on others for something as simple as a ride. "Don't worry about it. I'll manage."

"You have to have a ride." Terry obviously felt torn.

"I have to go into town later anyway," Nolie said. "I can easily drop you off."

She didn't want to make the offer, and he probably didn't want to accept it. Spending more time in the man's company was hardly the best way to get over the random attraction she'd imagined she felt. But she couldn't very well do anything else.

"Thanks, Nolie. That's great." Terry seemed to take her brother's acceptance for granted. "Gotta go." She barely waited until Nolie stepped back before she gunned the motor and went spinning out of the lane.

"Sorry." Gabe waved goodbye to Danny as they drove by more sedately. "My sister seems to have left her manners at home."

"It's fine. I'm happy to run you by the house when we've finished."

Another half hour in his company. Well, she'd figure out a way to deal with it. Maybe being around him would inoculate her against all that masculine energy.

"Thanks."

The word came out reluctantly, and she thought she knew why. Gabe didn't want to feel indebted to her for anything.

She started walking toward the training center, and he fell into step beside her. That faint limp was still there, audible if not visible to anyone who knew enough to pay attention to the rhythm of his steps.

"I hope you don't mind my introducing you to Danny. He asked to meet you."

"No problem. But why did he want to meet me?" He frowned. "You didn't tell him—"

"I didn't tell him about your seizure disorder." She used the words deliberately, hoping frequent use might rob them of some of their sting.

"Then why?"

"Surely you've run into that before. To a little kid, especially one like Danny who can't get around much, a firefighter is someone to look up to. I'm afraid he has a bad case of hero-worship."

She felt his steps halt, saw the tension drive lines deeper in his face. "He shouldn't," he said shortly.

He'd reacted before to that word. Maybe she'd better bring this out into the open. If they were to have any sort of a working relationship, she didn't want to keep tripping over things that bothered him.

"I've obviously said the wrong thing. Is it some sort of faux pas to refer to a firefighter as a hero—one of those things every firefighter knows?"

"No." His eyes had gone so dark they were almost black. "But if you want to call someone a hero, make it one of the firefighters who died in that warehouse fire. They were the heroes, not me."

Her breath caught at the pain etched into his words. He'd known those men who died, obviously. Still grieved for them. She reached toward him almost involuntarily, wanting to comfort him, not knowing how.

"I'm sorry." Her throat went tight on the words. "Sorry. I didn't mean to hurt you."

He shook his head, as if to shake off her sympathy. "Not your fault." He grasped her hands in both of his suddenly, and the sensation of his touch traveled straight up her arms in a warming wave, wiping out all the rational things she'd been saying to herself about the attraction she felt.

"Still, I—" Whatever she might have intended to say seemed to get lost in a welter of reaction.

"Look, I'm no hero. I'm just a man with a job to do. If you want to help me, make sure I go back to work. I'm over this seizure thing. I'm ready."

Her mind started to function again. He wanted her help, but not the help she was qualified to give.

"I'm sorry." She pulled her hands free. "It's not up to me. You know that."

"It could be." He didn't attempt to touch her again, but the intensity of his gaze nailed her to the spot. "The chief might listen to you if you told him I'm okay. That I'm ready to go back on the line."

He was grasping at straws, but she doubted he was ready to hear that.

"First things first." She tried to manage a cool smile. "We're here to do a job. Let's get on with that and put going back to work on the back burner for a while."

She thought he wanted to flare out at her, but he didn't. Instead he gave her a look she couldn't interpret. "I understand. You're right. Let's get started."

He turned toward the training center. She had to hurry to keep up, because her mind was spinning with possibilities.

What if Gabe was right about himself? If his seizures really were a thing of the past, he was no good to her as a test case. She had to get a handle on his physical condition, and soon.

And then there was the personal problem. What on

earth was she going to do with this totally inappropriate attraction she felt every time she was near the man?

He'd blown it. Gabe was still berating himself as Nolie put him and Max through a series of obedience exercises in the training center she'd set up in a converted garage. Her voice echoed through the wide space as she gave him directions. A barn swallow, apparently nesting in the rafters, swooped out the open door at the sound.

He shouldn't have rushed into telling her what he wanted. He should have taken it easy, let her warm up to him. Rationally presented his arguments.

Instead he'd blurted it out, making it almost inevitable that she'd say no.

He didn't intend to take Ryan's advice and try to charm the woman. Still, it wouldn't hurt to be friendly. Let her feel she was getting to know him. Get her on his side.

As for what he was going to do with that totally inappropriate blast of attraction he'd felt when he'd held her hands—well, that was probably a good thing to ignore. She wasn't his type. And at the moment, she was a very effective barrier to his getting what he wanted most in the world.

He and Max reached the end of the obstacle course. He waited for her to tell him what totally useless thing she wanted him to do next.

"Reward your dog," she reminded him in the same detached, calm tone she'd used the first four times she'd had to tell him that.

"Yes. Right." He gave the dog one of the treats Nolie had provided and patted him.

Nolie crossed the concrete floor to join them, frowning slightly.

"What?" She obviously thought he'd done something wrong. "I'm sorry I didn't remember."

"It's not that." She fondled Max's ears, and the dog looked up at her with a totally besotted expression of adoration. "Do you understand why I'm having you do obedience exercises with Max?"

He shrugged. He could hardly tell her again that he thought the whole thing was useless.

He thought she suppressed a sigh.

"Let's go out in the sun and take a break. There are some things you need to understand about the training."

Max stuck to Nolie's heels as if he were attached. He followed woman and dog outside.

An old-fashioned porch swing hung from the branch of an oak tree at the corner of the training center. Nolie sat and waited until he took the seat next to her. The swing creaked gently, swaying a little.

Nolie rubbed Max's head. "Max has already gone through obedience training. Haven't you, Maxie?"

He gave her a wide doggy grin.

"So the obedience training is for me." He said the obvious. She probably thought he needed a little obedience training.

A smile touched her face, softening it. The eyes he'd thought a pale, nondescript blue the day before had been turned to aqua by the sweater she had on.

"Not exactly. The training is for both of you. It's

to allow the two of you to get used to working together. More importantly, to let you bond with Max.''

He didn't need to bond with the dog, because they weren't going to be together that long. But now was probably not the time to say that. He ruffled the dog's fur, and Max leaned against his knee.

''He's a good-looking animal. Purebred?'' He'd show interest, not agreement.

''Max is mostly yellow lab, but I wouldn't venture a guess as to what the other part is. All my service dogs come from the humane society. They're abandoned animals who need a chance to prove they can be useful.''

She said that with a passion he didn't quite understand. There was a lot he didn't understand about Nolie, come to think of it.

''So, once Max and I have bonded to your satisfaction, what comes next?'' Supposing he had to stick around that long. ''What's your time frame?''

Worry lines creased her forehead. ''We only have a month. Still, I'm usually working with children, and it should go faster with an adult. I'd suggest that this week and next week we do obedience work and then put in two weeks of intensive live-in training.''

''Live-in? Not in the cottage?''

He glanced toward the cottage she'd shown him the day before. White frame with black shutters like the house. It had rosebushes on either side of the black front door. A yellow rambler rose was already coming into bloom on a trellis over the walk. It looked like a kid's playhouse.

''Yes, I know it's small, but I'm sure you'll do fine.'' The brisk assurance in her voice said that this was non-negotiable. "You and the dog have to live together during the intensive training. That twenty-four-hour-a-day experience is crucial to the whole process."

He got what she meant then, and he didn't like it. "You mean you're hoping I'll have a seizure during that time, don't you?"

"Not hoping, no." Her brows furrowed, and she seemed to choose her words carefully. "I hope you never have another one. But if you do, that's the test of whether Max will live up to my belief in him."

"There's no guarantee, in other words," he said flatly. "This could all be useless."

"It's not useless. I *can* guarantee you that when we've finished training together, Max will do his job in protecting you should a seizure occur. The question is whether he'll know the seizure is coming and warn you."

Passion for her work filled her as she said the words, so strong he almost felt its heat. The face he'd thought plain was alive with enthusiasm. He wanted to tell her again that he wasn't going to have another seizure, but she swept on.

"The foundation wanted scientific proof, and there isn't any. But it happens. I've seen it happen. When the bond between dog and client is strong enough, the dog knows when a seizure is coming."

He couldn't help being moved by the strength of her conviction. No one could. He leaned toward her, his hand on her shoulder, feeling the passion that flooded through her for her cause.

Nolie wanted to be sure a bond formed between him and the dog, so that she could prove her theories to the foundation. He wanted to create a bond between himself and Nolie, so that he could get her on his side.

The trouble was that if he sat this close to her for another moment, he'd probably kiss her. What would that do to either of their plans?

Chapter Four

Nolie walked through the chrome-and-glass doors of the fire-department administrative offices the next morning, trying to concentrate on the mission that had brought her here. Unfortunately her wayward imagination kept transporting her back to those moments on the swing with Gabe.

She'd given away too much of herself to him. She didn't do that with anyone except Claire, and that was only because she and Claire had found each other in a support group for abuse survivors.

The support group hadn't wiped away the dark shadows of her past, but it had given her an amazing friend. She was constantly grateful for that.

Claire was safe. She could tell Claire anything and know that it would never be used against her. But Gabe—

Gabe was so intent on his passion to return to fire fighting that she didn't think he'd stop at much to get there. Including using her, if he thought it would be to his advantage.

Had he seen, when she'd talked about the stray animals she trained, that she equated herself with those abandoned creatures? She had to find a way to keep her guard up with him, or he'd trample over her on his way back to the life he wanted.

And that wasn't the most serious problem. If Gabe continued to deny his need, that might keep him from bonding with his service dog. All her work on the grant proposal could come to nothing.

She crossed the glossy tile floor to the elevators, searching the posted directory for the fire chief's name. She had to get an unbiased opinion about Gabe, and she certainly couldn't get that from his family.

The Flanagan family's overflowing love would probably make them support him if he declared that the sky was pink with orange polka dots. She couldn't imagine what that must be like—to have people love and support you that much.

She stepped into the elevator, confronting her image in its mirrored wall. She wore the navy blazer again. Claire kept threatening to burn it, but she never did. Maybe she understood that Nolie needed the anonymity the blazer represented.

Worthless, her aunt's voice whispered in her memory.

Taking a breath, she concentrated on the blinking light that showed the floors. Whatever her aunt had believed, she wasn't worthless. She was doing good work, and she'd do even more once she had the grant. So she wasn't about to give up on Gabe Flanagan, no matter how much he'd like her to.

The elevator doors swished open, and she stepped into a long hallway, empty except for one person. Her stomach clenched. Brendan Flanagan. The Reverend Brendan Flanagan.

"Nolie, hi." His smile held a tinge of surprise. "What brings you here?"

She rejected the impulse to lie to him. "I wanted to speak with Chief Donovan. Is his office on this floor?"

Brendan nodded toward a door. "It is, but he isn't in right now. Can I help you?"

"I don't think so." Her grand plan seemed to be dissolving. "Maybe I can make an appointment to see him later."

He hesitated, his eyebrows lifting in a question. "Is this about Gabe?"

He wouldn't believe her if she said no. She nodded.

"Maybe I can help, unless it's something official." His smile was deprecating. "Even though I'm the department chaplain, they don't really trust me with official business."

He didn't look much like a chaplain in his rumpled khakis and navy pullover. He might be another of the young firefighters she'd seen downstairs.

"I really need to talk with someone about Gabe." She pushed her discomfort out of the way. This was too important to let her own hang-ups stop her. "Someone impartial."

He considered for a moment, weighing her words gravely. "Well, I'm not completely impartial. Gabe is my cousin, as well as my friend. But I think I can be objective about him." He smiled. "Unlike the rest of the Flanagans, I might add."

She managed a small smile in return. "They are certainly...supportive, I guess you could say."

"I'm not sure that's what Gabe would say, but it'll do." He gestured toward the end of the hall. "There's a break room here. I'll get you a cup of coffee, and you can tell me what you need to know about my cousin."

She didn't want to spend any more time than she had to in his company, but Brendan seemed genuine enough. And the prize she had to win was worth facing a few dragons, wasn't it?

"Thanks. I appreciate that."

The few minutes it took to settle themselves at a small table in the empty lounge let her organize her thoughts. She wrapped her fingers around the cup Brendan handed her and tried to look at him without thinking of him as a minister.

It was easier than she'd have expected, probably because he didn't look like any minister she'd ever met, not that she'd met that many. Brother Joshua had been enough for a lifetime.

"What can I tell you about Gabe?" Brendan pushed back the lock of dark hair that tumbled toward the rims of his glasses.

She reconsidered her view of him. With his serious, studious expression and his glasses, he looked more like a young professor than either a firefighter or a minister.

"I'm trying to find the best way to work with Gabe," she said carefully. She had to keep in mind that this was Gabe's cousin. "So far I'm finding that he's—"

She stopped. Too attractive for his own good? Too

appealing to be alone with? She didn't want to go there.

"In complete denial," Brendan said.

She gave him a look of surprised gratitude. "Yes, he is. I thought I was the only one who saw that."

Brendan frowned down at the dark coffee in his cup. "Siobhan does, I think, but probably no one else in the family. As for the chief—well, I know he has a desk job lined up for Gabe, in the event he can't go back on active duty."

She turned that over in her mind, wondering. "Do you think Gabe would accept that?"

"Not for a minute."

This time his answer didn't surprise her.

"He's certainly determined to get back to work. So much so that I'm afraid it's influencing his attitude toward working with me."

Brendan grinned. "You mean he's so bullheaded that he can't see anything but his own objective."

"Something like that."

"You have to understand." He leaned across the table toward her, eyes intent. "Gabe's a warrior. Always has been. An old-fashioned knight in shining armor rushing to rescue the helpless. That's what being a firefighter means to him."

The image warmed her. "You care a lot about him."

"Like a brother. All Flanagans have fire fighting in the blood, but Gabe most of all." His brows drew together. "The thing is, if Gabe can't be a firefighter—" He stopped and shook his head, his eyes dark and serious. "If Gabe can't be a firefighter, I don't think he'll know who he is."

* * *

Brendan's words were still ringing in Nolie's ears as she set up an obstacle course on the lawn behind the house later in the afternoon. That conversation had gone a lot better than she'd expected, on several counts.

She'd gotten over her instinctive need to escape from him. She hadn't even winced when he'd taken her hand and told her he'd be praying for her.

And he'd given her a glimmer of an idea. His description of Gabe as a knight rescuing the helpless had clicked into place. Of course that's what he was—a modern-day knight. She just had to find a way of working his need to help and rescue into his training.

She tested the white picket gate she'd set up, making sure it was stable. Max nosed against it, as if remembering his lessons, then trotted off to join Lady in investigating an interesting smell under the willow tree. A bee buzzed lazily past her toward the old-fashioned lilac bush next to the back porch, and the lilac's aroma perfumed the air.

A perfect spring day—meant for lazing in a hammock, not indulging in a case of the nerves over what she had to do. She heard one car pull into the lane, and then another, and took a deep, settling breath.

Please, let this work. It would be so good for Gabe and for Danny. Please.

Her thoughts flitted to the grant. It could mean the difference between expanding her work and going under. Deep down she probably didn't really trust anyone, but like it or not, she needed Gabe.

Repeating the prayer in her heart, she headed toward the lane to greet her clients. She waved at Danny, then nodded to Gabe as he got out of the car. In jeans, a polo shirt and sneakers, he looked ready to work. She hoped.

"Hi. Would you mind helping Danny's mother get him out of the car?"

"Of course not." He swung toward them automatically, then glanced at her, frowning. "Did I have the time wrong today?"

"No. I just thought you and Danny might benefit from working together a few times."

His frown lingered as he seemed to assess her words. Her heart gave a little thump. If he knew what she was up to—

That was silly. She bent to greet Gabe's mother.

"Hi, Mrs. Flanagan. Did you want to wait for Gabe?"

"Call me Siobhan, please." Her warm smile crinkled the faint lines around her eyes. "Actually, I was hoping you might bring him home and stay for supper with us. I promise not to inflict all the Flanagans on you this time."

Ordinarily she'd accept any invitation that would allow her insight into a client, but Gabe was different.

He's a client, the voice of her conscience pointed out. You should treat him as you would any client.

That was certainly easier said than done.

"Gabe might have had enough of me by that time."

"Gabe doesn't always know what's good for him." Siobhan had a note of determination in her voice. "Please, Nolie." She put her hand on Nolie's where it rested on the edge of the window. "I really want you to come."

For Gabe's sake. Siobhan didn't say that, but that

was what she meant. Well, if she were honest with herself about putting the client first, she could hardly refuse.

"Thanks. I'd like that." And if she succeeded in tapping into Gabe's need to help others, she might have something to celebrate by then.

"What are you two plotting?"

The low bass rumble of Gabe's voice resonated through her, and she felt instantly guilty.

"Nothing. Your mother was just kind enough to invite me to supper."

"She was?" He bent to give his mother a look that should have singed, but Siobhan just smiled at him serenely. He lifted his hand in what might have been a gesture of either goodbye or surrender. "I'll see you later, Mom."

Siobhan waved, then put the car in gear and moved off. Gabe turned that smoldering look on Nolie, jolting her down to her bones.

"Mind telling me what's going on?"

"What makes you think something is going on?"

"You've obviously scheduled me for the same time as Danny. I want to know why."

She tried to pull her professional expertise around her like a cloak. She was the expert. She didn't have to explain herself to him.

"Because I think it would be good for both of you to work together today."

Danny's approach kept Gabe from giving the stinging response that was undoubtedly on his tongue, but his burning glance told her clearly what he thought of this idea.

Brendan, you'd better be right about him. With a

whispered prayer, she led the man and boy toward the lawn.

By the time they'd put in a half hour's work, she had finally begun to relax. It looked as if Brendan *had* been right. No matter how reluctant Gabe was, his protective instincts kicked in once he was actually working with the boy. She could read it in his body language as he leaned toward Danny while boy and dog worked on operating the gate.

"You can do it, Danny." Gabe's fingers twitched with the longing to open the gate for the boy, but he clearly realized the need for Danny to do it himself.

"Sure you can." She added her words of encouragement. "Just let Lady do most of the work for you."

Danny's small face tightened in concentration as he tried to force recalcitrant nerves to carry the message to his hands. Lady, eager to help, nosed at the latch.

Nolie held her breath as the gate swung a millimeter open. If it snapped back again—

This time Danny pulled out of the way and let Lady have her head. The dog, concentrating almost as fiercely as the boy, shouldered the gate open and held it. Danny wheeled through.

"We did it!" The triumph in Danny's voice grabbed her heart and squeezed.

"You sure did, buddy." Gabe gave him a thumbs-up sign.

He glanced at Nolie. For a moment they were completely in sync, sharing a potent mix of joy and triumph. Gabe's eyes darkened, as if in recognition. As if he and Nolie were seeing each other for the first time and knew this was no casual meeting.

Breathe, she admonished herself. She couldn't let the man touch her emotions that way.

"Now you," Danny said, his eyes shining as he looked up at his hero. "You and Max should work the gate, too."

Gabe hesitated, and she knew he was thinking that he didn't need to accomplish that task in the same way that wheelchair-bound Danny did.

"That's right," she said quickly. "Max has been taught how to work the gate. It's a good exercise. See if you can do it together."

He nodded, tapping his leg to call Max to heel. Together they approached the gate.

"Don't try to do all the work." Danny's words mimicked what she'd said so often to him. "Let Max help you do it."

Gabe reached for the gate, then slowed, moving as he'd seen Danny move. He hesitated.

"You can do it, Gabe," Danny said. "You can."

Gabe's lips twitched at the boy's coaching, but he nodded. "Open the gate, Max."

It was the first time he'd given the dog a verbal command without her prompting, and she smiled. Gabe might not realize it, but he was making progress.

Max glanced up at Gabe, apparently looking for confirmation. Then he nosed the latch, helping Gabe release it. He caught the gate with his shoulder, just as she'd taught him. Man and dog passed through smoothly.

"Good job, Max!" Again, Danny's words were an echo of hers. He struggled to make his hand give the same thumbs-up signal Gabe had.

She glanced from Danny to Gabe, and her gaze was

caught by Gabe's face as he bent over, ruffling Max's fur and murmuring to the dog.

Her heart clenched. They were bonding. Gabe could say a dozen times a day that he didn't need the dog, but they'd just taken the first step toward becoming a partnership.

And when they did, they'd also taken the first step away from her.

She tried to smooth over the pricking thought. Letting go was the nature of her work. She'd accepted that a long time ago. She trained them, encouraged them, even loved them, and then they went away. Gabe would do that, too.

That shouldn't matter to her any more than it would with any other client, but she feared it would.

Gabe smoothed the dog's silky ears, then ran his hand down Max's shoulder, feeling strong muscle and bone. One might almost think the dog enjoyed working and felt a sense of accomplishment in what he did. As Gabe did.

He glanced at Nolie. Danny had wheeled over to her, and she bent toward the boy, congratulating him. The face he'd once thought plain was lit with pride in the child's accomplishment, maybe even love.

His stomach seemed to turn over. Why on earth had he thought her plain? She was beautiful.

Okay, back up. He couldn't go around thinking things like that. He had no intention of getting close to either Nolie or Danny. Period. So he would not notice Nolie's quick graceful movements, or the way her skin turned golden where the sun touched it. And he wouldn't let his heart twist with longing to make things better for the kid.

It was probably a good thing that the boy's mother arrived just then to pick him up. He watched as Nolie took Danny to the car, exchanging a few words with the mother as they loaded him in.

He raised his hand in farewell to the boy, and then frowned as Nolie strolled back to him.

"Doesn't his father ever bring Danny?"

Quick sorrow filled her expressive face. "Danny's parents are separated. Lately it seems they quarrel about everything, including Danny's therapy. So no, his dad doesn't ever bring him." She raised her hand to wave away a bee that buzzed near her face. "It's hard on parents, having a child with as many disabilities as Danny does."

"It's pretty hard on the kid, too." He couldn't help the edge of anger in his voice. "I don't have much use for people who can't put their child first."

The flash of pain in her eyes at his words startled him. Was some personal experience at work there?

He wouldn't ask about her family. He wasn't going to get involved, remember?

The moment passed. Nolie started taking down the portable gate and he moved to help her, taking the supports as she dismantled them.

"Thanks."

She carried the gate toward the barn, and he followed, lugging the supports. They crossed the grass and moved from sunlight into the cool, dim interior of the barn.

It was quiet. Peaceful. There wasn't much quiet in his life at the moment, and this felt good.

Nolie stacked the gate pieces she carried against an empty stall. He shoved his into place.

"Danny's doing well, in spite of his parents." Nolie glanced at him, as if measuring her words. "He's a hard worker normally, but he worked even harder today, thanks to you."

"I didn't do anything."

"You made him feel—" She paused, searching for the words. "Well, maybe not quite so exceptional. Not so alone. Having someone else here made it almost a game for him."

"He's a brave little kid." He couldn't imagine facing the future the boy faced every day.

She smiled. "He looks up to you."

Hero-worship, that was what she was talking about. The phrase turned the screws on him. A real hero wouldn't still be walking around when two of his comrades were dead.

They stepped out into the sunlight again, and he raised his hand to shield his eyes. Lady and Max, chasing each other on the lawn, broke off the game to come racing over to them, jostling each other for Nolie's attention.

She laughed and patted her shoulder, obviously an invitation to Max. The dog reared up and planted two big paws on her shoulders, and she hugged him. Her hair, touched by the sun, was almost the same gold as the dog's fur.

"That dog's a lover, not a fighter," he said.

She shoved Max down gently, still smiling, and ruffled Lady's ears. Max, apparently deciding on second-best, came to lean against Gabe's leg and have his ears rubbed.

"Max is special. Well, they all are, I guess."

For the first time he wondered at her attachment. "You obviously love them."

"Well, of course." She looked surprised.

"How do you handle parting with them?"

Her lashes swept down, hiding her eyes from him. Hiding her emotions, probably.

"It's hard." She patted Lady. "But that's what success means in my business. Partnering the right animal with the right client, and saying goodbye when they're ready to be on their own."

"It sounds kind of lonely, when you put it like that."

She shrugged. "I've gotten used to it."

She almost sounded as if she believed that. Almost, but not quite.

They'd reached the front of the farmhouse, and he looked up at the sign that hung there. It was wooden, brightly painted, showing an ark with fanciful animals poking their noses out of doors and windows. Nolie's Ark, it read in script around the edge.

"Very appropriate," he commented.

She smiled, and a faint flush touched her cheeks. "I'd have put up something much more serious and formal, but my friend Claire beat me to it. She said if I had to turn this place into an ark, I might as well have a sign to match."

"She's a good friend."

"Yes, she is." The smile lingered on her lips at the thought of her friend.

Did she smile when she mentioned him in conversation? Probably not. He'd managed to turn himself into a pretty big thorn in her side in a few short days.

"Well." She put her hand on the porch railing. "I'd like to change before I take you home, if I'm staying for supper." She gestured toward the faded jeans she wore. "Do you mind waiting?"

The reminder of his dependence pricked. "I don't have much choice, do I?"

She stopped on the step, turning toward him, and their faces were level. She was so close he could see the fine sheen of sunlight on her cheek, the tiny veins at her temples, the flecks of gold in her eyes. How had he ever thought her plain? He must have been out of his mind.

"I'm sorry. I know you must hate being driven." Her smile flickered. "It's tough to give up control, isn't it?"

He shrugged, annoyed that she saw through him so clearly. "It won't be for long. When I've gone six months without a seizure, the doc says I'll get my license back."

"Good." She said it as if she meant it, but he knew better.

His hand tightened on the railing. "Is it, Nolie? If I don't have a seizure in six months, that won't do your grant proposal much good, will it?"

He saw by the flicker in her eyes that the shot had gone home. But she lifted her chin, looking at him steadily.

"I know you don't believe this, but we really want the same thing. We both want you to be able to live your life as fully and richly as possible, whether that means you're going to be doing that with a seizure-alert animal or not."

Not. I choose not. The thought burned into his brain.

The trouble was that he might not have the ability to choose.

Nolie lingered a moment longer, as if waiting for him to respond to her words. Then, with what might have been a sigh, she went into the house.

They didn't want the same thing, no matter how much Nolie might like to believe that. He wouldn't live his life depending on an animal to take care of him. He'd go back to the work he was destined to do. Nolie could help him, or she could be an obstacle, but he was going to do it.

Chapter Five

Nolie took the flowered plate Siobhan had just put into the dish rack and polished it with a linen tea towel. She'd practically had to strong-arm Gabe's mother to be allowed to help with the cleaning up after dinner.

The heavy gold of Siobhan's wedding ring hit the edge of a china plate, setting off a soft pealing, like a very small bell. Siobhan smiled, faint lines crinkling at the corners of her eyes.

"This is nice—doing the dishes together. The kids always badger me about using the dishwasher, but I like the feel of the hot soapy water. It takes me back to doing the dishes with my mother."

Since Nolie didn't have any such positive memories of her own mother, she couldn't very well contribute to that subject. She'd have to say something else.

"It was nice of you to invite me to supper. I'd have been glad to drive Gabe even without the bribe of a home-cooked meal, though."

Siobhan's laugh was as soft and clear as that peal of ring against plate. "I'm too used to my own mob. You can get just about anything by bribing Flanagans with food."

"I'll remember that. Maybe I should start offering Gabe treats, the way I do the dog."

Siobhan's hands stilled, and she seemed to be looking through the window above the sink, across the darkening lawn toward the lights of the houses on the next street.

"I don't want you to break any confidences, but I'd love to know how he's doing."

How was Gabe doing? Her memory flashed to those moments when they'd been in such complete accord in their compassion for Danny. For a brief space of time she'd imagined they were partners, joined together in a common cause.

But they weren't. The moment had shattered on the rock of Gabe's inability to accept her goals for him.

She'd been quiet too long. She had to say something.

"It's not a matter of confidentiality." She put a plate neatly on the stack. Siobhan had a point. There was something soothing about the quiet routine and the accompanying chime of women's voices. "I'd be delighted if I could tell you it's going well."

"But it's not."

She shook her head, trying to find the right words to express her frustration. Gabe's father had made his opinion of her work clear, but maybe Siobhan would help, if Nolie just knew how to explain.

"Gabe holds back," she said finally. "He doesn't want to depend on the dog, and as long as he feels that way, it will be difficult for a bond to form. Gabe thinks it's unnecessary. He believes he'll never have another seizure.''

Siobhan nodded, running her hands absently along the curve of a bowl. ''I pray that all the time, but that may not be God's plan for Gabe.''

''Unfortunately, Gabe doesn't seem able to look at any future except going back to fire fighting.''

''They're all mad about it.'' Siobhan's hands tightened, gripping the bowl so hard her fingers turned white. ''I wish—''

She stopped, as if whatever she wished were somehow disloyal.

Nolie touched Siobhan's hand, warm from the dishwater. ''You worry about them, don't you?''

''Nonsense.''

The booming voice made both of them jump. She turned to see Gabe's father, closely followed by Gabe. She'd been so intent on her conversation with Siobhan that she hadn't heard their approach.

''Nonsense,'' Joe said again, crossing the faded kitchen linoleum to put his arm around Siobhan's still-slender waist and hug her close. ''Siobhan's a true firefighter's wife. She knows we'll all be fine. Flanagans are lucky. Look at Gabe, walking away from that accident.''

Did he really believe what he was saying? She glanced at Gabe, her heart giving a little jolt when she realized his eyes were on her. Did Gabe believe it?

''You'd better be lucky.'' Siobhan patted Joe's cheek. ''I'm not about to get along without you.''

The love between them was so palpable it hit Nolie

like a blow. Had her parents ever had that kind of feeling for each other? If they had, it hadn't lasted.

Her eyes suddenly stung with tears, and she blinked them back furiously. She hadn't cried about her parents in years. She certainly wasn't going to let the Flanagans, with that aura they had of loving and being loved, make her remember.

She hung the tea towel on the rack. "Well, I'd better be getting back to the farm. My animals will want their supper, too. Thank you again for the delicious meal."

"You're welcome any time." Siobhan surprised her with a quick hug. "In fact, why don't you come along to church with us on Sunday and have dinner afterward? You'd enjoy hearing Brendan preach."

"No. Thank you." She hoped that didn't sound too abrupt. "I already have plans for Sunday with a friend, but thanks just the same."

"Another time, then."

She nodded, not meaning it. Being pulled into the Flanagan family loop was difficult enough, with its reminders of all she'd never had. She wasn't about to get dragged to a church service with them.

"I'll walk you out to the car."

The offer, in the low rumble of Gabe's voice, startled her. She'd thought he'd be only too glad to be rid of her.

But he walked beside her out the back door and down the porch steps. Their footsteps were muted by the grass as they crossed the lawn to where her car was parked in front of the garage.

The spring twilight sent shadows reaching across

the grass from the mature shrubs and trees. An old tire swing moved slightly in the breeze.

Permanence. The Flanagan house exuded an air of having been here always, of planning to stay forever, sheltering its people with love and security.

"It's quiet here." The neighborhood street wasn't as quiet as the farm, of course, but it wasn't as noisy as she'd have expected. The tall sentinels of yews formed a barricade along the edge of the property, lending an air of seclusion.

"Not too quiet." Gabe nodded toward the street, and when she listened, she could hear the faint sound of children's voices.

"They're out late."

Gabe glanced at his watch. "It still gets dark fairly early. They'll all be watching for the street lights to come on. That's the signal that it's time to come in."

Come in, he'd said, as if he were one of those children playing hide and seek between the houses.

"That's what you did."

He smiled. "Of course. Didn't you?"

"We didn't have street lights in the country."

And I didn't have the kind of childhood that seems so normal to you.

But she wouldn't say that to him. She didn't tell people. She didn't want their pity making her weak.

She fumbled for her keys as they reached the car, but Gabe seemed in no hurry for her to leave. He propped one large hand against the roof of the car.

"So what was your signal to come in from playing?"

"I don't remember." She didn't remember because

there hadn't been any. Because there hadn't been any playtime.

"Come now." He brushed a strand of hair back from her face. His knuckle grazed her cheek and set up a path of heat where it touched. "A pretty little blonde like you must have attracted every boy in the county to come and play."

Vanity. Brother Joshua's voice boomed in her head. *That hair is an invitation to vanity for the child. And a temptation to men.*

She slammed the door on the ugly voice. She wouldn't let a dark memory destroy this moment of closeness with Gabe.

"My aunt was very strict." That was certainly a masterpiece of understatement.

"My dad was strict, too, but there was always time to play." His touch lingered, warming her.

"You were lucky." The words were out before she thought about what they might betray. "I mean, you had brothers and sisters to play with, even when there weren't other kids around."

"The Flanagans have always been a tribe," he said. "With Mom cheering us on and Dad telling us what to do."

"He still does, doesn't he?" That was an even worse slip. The warmth of his hand against her face robbed her of the ability to be even moderately tactful.

Gabe didn't actually move, but he seemed to withdraw. "He's our father. We all respect his opinion."

She'd already destroyed the temporary bond between them. She may as well say the rest of what she thought. "Even when he says your mother doesn't worry? Or that you'll be back at work in no time?"

His face hardened, and his hand dropped away from her cheek, leaving her skin chilled where the warmth had been. "You don't know anything about my relationship with my father. He's expressing his faith in me."

"You're right. I don't know about your relationship with him." And she certainly didn't have any experience of her own to guide her.

"Well, then—"

"But I know something about adjusting to disabilities. And I can see that your father won't admit the extent of your injury because it would mean admitting his own mortality, too."

If Gabe had put his hands on her and pushed her away, he couldn't have rejected her words more completely. He folded his arms across his chest, maybe because otherwise he really would have pushed her away.

"Leave my family out of it. I make my own decisions about what I do."

She was making a mess of this, but she had to try. "I can't leave them out. Their attitude influences you. When you bring Max home with you, they'll be involved."

"No. They won't." His face was a hardened mask, shutting her out. "Because that's not going to happen. You can play all the games you want with Danny and the dogs, but it won't change a thing. I don't need what you're offering."

He really believed that. Her throat tightened until she could barely speak.

"I'm sorry you feel that way." She forced the

words out. "For your sake, I hope you're right about your needs. But I don't think you are."

Gabe took a step back from the car. She yanked the door open. She'd destroyed enough for one night. She'd better get out before she made things any worse.

Gabe had come to the farm still annoyed with Nolie on Monday, but by the end of the session, he'd managed to cool off. He shouldn't have let himself get so upset by Nolie's comments about his family. She clearly didn't know anything about families. Maybe that aunt that she'd mentioned living with had been her only relative.

They'd been working inside the training center today, and he stood back, absently fondling Max's ears, while Nolie talked to Danny about what they'd done. Both Danny and Lady seemed to listen with equal intensity.

He had himself in hand now, and he knew what he had to do. He'd go through with the training, because he didn't have a choice. Three more weeks of it, and then he'd be finished. Then he'd tell Nolie goodbye, go to the captain and demand his job back.

Nolie and Danny turned to head out the door and he fell into step beside them. Nolie shot him a questioning look. He responded with a noncommittal smile. After all, there were worse ways to spend a sick leave than walking in the sunshine with a pretty woman, even if that woman was totally wrong-headed about everything.

"Good session today, Danny." He rested his hand on the boy's shoulder as they walked toward Danny's mother, waiting by her car. "It was fun to work together."

"I bet you'd have more fun if you were at the fire station with the other firefighters."

He tried to suppress the pain that clutched him at the kid's innocent words. Danny couldn't know how that hurt him.

"Well, sometimes it's fun. And some of the guys are pretty good cooks. We all have to take turns at that."

"You do?" The kid's eyes were big. "Do you really slide down a pole when the alarm goes off?"

"Every time," he said solemnly. All right, this wasn't so hard. He'd answered these kinds of questions from kids dozens of times. There was no reason to tense up.

"Wish I could go to the fire station." Danny's tone was wistful.

He wished the same. But he had no intention of going as a visitor. He'd go when he was ready to go back on duty, not before.

"It's a pretty busy place," he said.

He caught Nolie's look and returned it with an annoyed one of his own. She was obviously thinking that he should offer to take the kid to the station. Well, she'd just have to go on thinking it, because he wouldn't offer.

"Mom was sorry you couldn't go to church with us yesterday." Let her feel guilty about what she hadn't done, instead of trying to load guilt onto him.

For an instant she looked startled at the change of subject, and then her eyes narrowed. She got his point, all right.

"I spent the day with my friend, Claire. You met her."

He nodded, remembering the woman who'd seemed such an odd friend for Nolie to have. "Did you—"

He stopped, frowning at the tan SUV that spun into the lane, kicking up gravel as it stopped abruptly behind Danny's mother's van. Someone was in a hurry.

The soft intake of Nolie's breath was almost a gasp. He looked at her to see that her face had paled.

"What is it?"

"Nothing." She managed a smile, but it looked frozen.

"What's my dad doing here?" Danny sounded apprehensive.

All Gabe's hackles went up. Something wasn't right. The kid's father charged out of his car, slamming the door.

"Gabe, would you take Danny in the house for a drink?" Nolie's voice was calm, but her eyes showed strain. "There's a pitcher of lemonade in the fridge, and some cookies on the counter."

He shot a look toward the man. He was saying something they couldn't hear to his wife, but whatever it was, it didn't look pleasant.

"Maybe I'd better stay," he said softly.

She shook her head. "I can handle it. Take Danny inside. Please," she added.

Presumably she knew best about this. He grabbed the wheelchair handles and began pushing the boy toward the ramp that led up to the farmhouse porch.

"Let's go get some of that lemonade, okay?"

The skin on the back of his neck prickled as they went up the ramp, but there was no explosion of voices behind him. Nolie had said she could handle it, but he wasn't so sure. A big, angry man might be too much for her. Still, Max had glued himself to her side, and the man would have to be stupid to take on that dog.

"Okay." He held the screen door open and pushed the wheelchair into the kitchen. "Where's that lemonade?"

"And cookies," Danny added.

Given the obvious age of the farmhouse, he was a little surprised to find the kitchen had been completely modernized with sleek birch cabinetry and a sweep of white tile floor. Baskets hung from an exposed beam, and white curtains framed the windows.

"Lemonade and cookies coming right up."

He grabbed a couple of glasses from the dish drainer and took the pitcher from the fridge, keeping half his attention on Danny and half on the scene that was unfolding outside. The kid's father was obviously outraged about something. At the slightest sign the scene was going to turn physical, he'd be out the door in a split second.

But nothing happened. He kept Danny distracted with tales of riding the fire truck, sirens screaming, while he glanced out the window every few seconds. Nolie was, as she'd said, handling it. At least, he guessed she was. After a few minutes' worth of arm-waving, the man slammed his way into his SUV and spun back out of the lane.

"Looks like your mom is coming in for you now." He managed a more genuine smile. The crisis was over, apparently. "How about another cookie for the road?"

Whatever they were feeling, both Nolie and the

boy's mother managed to smile when they came inside. Nodding her thanks, the mother seized the wheelchair and headed back out the door immediately.

"Bye, Gabe. Bye, Nolie. See you next time." Danny waved as his chair rolled down the ramp.

Nolie waved back, smiling, but he could see the strain in the lines around her eyes and the tightness of her mouth.

"I'm sorry," he said, once they were gone. "Was it a bad scene?"

She shook her head, as if trying to shake off the feelings brought on by the encounter. "Not too bad. I think I told you Danny's parents were separated."

"Not an amicable separation, obviously." He handed her a glass of the lemonade.

"No." Tears filled her eyes. "That poor child. He loves them both. Don't they see that they're tearing him apart?"

The note of anguish that filled her voice struck him right in the heart. Of course she cared about Danny, but her pain went deeper than that. It almost sounded as if she were talking about herself.

"Is that what your parents did to you?"

The question was out before he thought about how personal it was. She'd probably tell him to mind his own business. That was pretty much what he'd told her about his family, after all.

"N-no." Her voice shook. "I was talking about Danny, not me." She put up one hand to brush her hair back away from her face, and the hand shook, too.

"Were you?" He touched her arm lightly, feeling

the tension that vibrated through her. "Seems like you identify with the kid's situation pretty closely."

"Anyone would." Her anger covered pain, but didn't quite hide it. "You don't have to have experienced it to feel for him."

"You and I are not friends," he said carefully. "You don't have to tell me anything. But I know what my instincts are telling me. And they're saying that you've got a history something like Danny's."

Nolie glared at Gabe for an instant longer. She'd like to be angry with him. She'd like to tell him to mind his own business.

Unfortunately, he was right. She shook her head, her anger seeping away, leaving her chilled. "You have pretty good instincts, it seems to me."

Gabe leaned back against the counter, his body language inviting her to talk.

She didn't tell people about her past. She certainly didn't want to confide in a client.

Still, Gabe's solid presence was oddly reassuring. She'd been aware of that presence the whole time she was dealing with Danny's father, knowing that if she'd needed him, Gabe would have been there.

There was no explaining that kind of knowledge. It simply was. She'd known Gabe for a week, but she had no doubt about that. His urge to protect would never let him stand back when someone was in need.

"My parents separated when I was two, I think," she said carefully. "And again when I was three and four and five. Even at that age, the quarrels were memorable. I know how it affected me. I hate to see it happening to Danny."

"Sounds like your situation was even worse." His voice was a low, sympathetic murmur.

"I'm not sure you can quantify something like that." She wrapped her arms around herself. She needed something to hold on to whenever she thought about the past. "Usually, when my father left, my mother would dump me with anybody she could find who'd take me."

Gabe reached out a long arm and pulled her closer, so that she was leaning against the counter next to him. His arm around her was a lot stronger, a lot more reassuring, than hugging herself.

"Then she'd take you back again?"

She nodded. "We'd play at being a happy family for a while. Then it would happen all over again."

He ran his hand up and down on her arm, the movement as soothing as stroking one of the dogs. "You told me the other day that an aunt raised you."

She'd told him too much, but she couldn't seem to back away. It was entirely too comforting to feel the warmth of his tough, strong body next to her. To hear the sympathy in his voice.

"Eventually they decided they were better off without a kid complicating things. So my mother got the bright idea of dropping me off here with my great-aunt. She figured Aunt Mariah's ideas of duty wouldn't let her turn me away. But she took the precaution of pinning a note to my jacket and dropping me off at the end of the lane."

The look on Gabe's face was thunderous. "She should have been tossed in jail. They both should have."

She shrugged. "They didn't want to be parents. I was in the way."

"No kid should ever feel in the way."

She pictured the children she'd seen the night she'd had dinner with the Flanagans. In that family, children were cherished. What must that be like, never questioning that you were loved?

"Well, at least my mother was right about Aunt Mariah. She didn't kick me out."

She could feel his gaze on her face, probing. "Judging by the tone of your voice, I'd say that situation wasn't exactly happily ever after."

He was never going to know just how bad it had been. "My great-aunt didn't want a kid, either, but at least I was fed and clothed. And I had the animals to love. That made a difference."

Was she sounding pitiful? She certainly didn't mean it that way. Having the animals to take care of and love had saved her.

She looked up at Gabe, wanting to explain that, so he wouldn't think he had to pity her. But somehow the explanations got lost on their way to her lips.

Gabe's face was very close, and those deep blue eyes were so dark they were almost black with emotion. She could see the faint stubble on his jaw, the crease next to his mouth, the cleft of his chin. His breath touched her face.

For an instant neither of them moved, but it seemed that their breaths mingled in wordless speech. Then she moved—or he moved—and their lips met.

Warmth. He was so warm. If she were just close enough to him, she'd never be cold again. Gabe's arms closed around her, and the room went spinning away. The world narrowed down to the circle of his arms.

She'd wanted this from the first time they'd met, she recognized through a haze of longing. It didn't make any sense, but it felt right. His arms around her felt right. If she'd ever imagined that she could care about a man enough to let him get this close, it would be someone like Gabe—someone strong and brave and caring.

Gabe's lips moved to her cheek, incredibly gentle. "Nolie." He said her name on a soft exhalation of breath that caressed her skin.

Then, as if the sound of his own voice had roused him from a dream, he pulled away. She could only stare up at him, knowing she must look as confused as he did.

Then his eyes lost the confused look. Now they were just appalled.

"I'm sorry." His voice was a husky whisper. "I don't know quite how that happened."

Neither did she. She swallowed hard and then forced herself to take a step away from him.

"It's all right." She shook her head. "I'm afraid there was a little too much emotion floating around this kitchen."

He looked relieved at that suggestion, as if she'd just handed him a way out of an impossible situation. "Guess so. Anyway, I'm sorry."

She couldn't let him see that his embrace meant anything more to her than it had to him.

"It was just a kiss." There wasn't anything "just" about it.

"Right." He took another backward step. "Well,

I—'' He looked out the window, and the air of relief increased. ''Looks like my ride is here. I'd better get going.''

Fleeing, she thought as he hurried out the door. Gabe was escaping.

She couldn't blame him. Any relationship between them was out of the question, and they both knew it.

Now all she had to do was convince herself to forget that kiss, and she'd be fine. Just fine.

Chapter Six

He was looking at a coward. Gabe stared at his image in the mirror as he shaved. A coward. He could face a wall of fire, but he couldn't face a woman's pain. He'd run away from Nolie.

What's more, he'd spent the rest of the week pretending it hadn't happened. He'd acted as if Nolie hadn't exposed her painful past to him, as if he hadn't been drawn to her, as if he hadn't kissed her.

Unfortunately, pretending didn't make it so.

Since Monday, he'd been carefully cooperative, showing up for his sessions every day, doing exactly what Nolie suggested. He'd worked with Danny each time. Maybe Nolie had arranged it that way because she was just as happy as he was to have the protection of a third party.

That protection was about to vanish, though. He rubbed his face with a towel, and then pulled a polo shirt over his head. This was Saturday, the day appointed for his move to the farm to begin his intensive training.

From now on he'd be seeing Nolie constantly, most of the time without the buffer Danny provided. They were both going to have to learn to deal with that.

He crossed the bedroom and grabbed his duffel bag. Nolie would be by to pick him up soon.

He seemed to see again her face, vulnerable and open to him when she'd told her story. His heart clenched. He suspected very few people had ever heard what she'd told him. And he'd responded by running away.

Why on earth hadn't her parents put Nolie up for adoption if they didn't want to take care of her? Some childless couple would have lavished on Nolie all the love and cherishing she deserved. Instead she'd been tossed around like a toy no one wanted.

Nolie had grown up alone, lonely, unwanted. She'd had to give all the love she'd stored up to the animals. Meanwhile he'd had more love and more family than he deserved. They might drive him crazy sometimes, but he never doubted their love.

He glanced at the photographs on the walls—pictures of him with his brothers and sisters, of ballgames, picnics, camping trips, family reunions. Family.

His gaze zeroed in on a photo of Ryan, taken at the end of his firefighter training. Head flung back, laughing as if he didn't have a care in the world.

Ryan was taking unnecessary risks, and something had to be done about it. He'd tried talking to Dad, but that had done no good. The old man had just laughed and told him he was worrying too much. Maybe Dad thought he was fussing about Ryan because of his own close shave.

Nolie's crazy theory about Dad popped into his head, and he shrugged it off. She didn't understand. Still, if Dad didn't see how serious this business with Ryan could be, it was up to him. One more reason why he had to get back on the line, and soon.

He picked up the container of seizure medication from the bedside table. He should be taking one now. He balanced the plastic container on his palm. Should be. But he'd never get back on active duty while he was on the meds. So maybe it was time to start weaning himself off them.

Tossing the unopened bottle into his bag, he started down the stairs.

Voices from the living room told him Nolie was already here. Arranging his face in a smile, he jogged down the steps to meet her.

"Right on time, I see."

Nolie nodded a greeting to him, her expression coolly detached.

If this situation bothered her, she certainly wouldn't show it. The trouble was that he now knew enough about her history to understand those barriers she kept in place.

"We can stop by your apartment and pick up anything else you need, and then you'll have time to get settled at the cottage before we get in a session this afternoon."

Mom handed him a shopping bag. "I put some food together for you. So you won't have to worry about getting groceries in right away."

"You didn't have to do that."

Ryan came through from the kitchen, jacket in hand, on his way out to work. "Relax, Mom. He's not going to Siberia. Hi, Nolie."

Siobhan grabbed Ryan's arm and planted a kiss on his cheek. "You be careful, now."

"Hey, that's no fun." Ryan hugged her.

"Be careful anyway," Gabe said, frowning at his brother. He'd like to say more, but he couldn't, not in front of their mother.

"Take care, bro." Ryan's expression mocked him. "You, too, Nolie." He went on out the door.

"That boy." His mother's expression was indulgent. "He always has to have the last word."

"Time he got over that. He's not six any more, even though he acts it sometimes."

His mother patted Gabe's cheek, and he thought she suppressed the urge to tell him to be a good boy. "We'll pick you up for church in the morning." She turned to Nolie. "We'd love to have you join us, too."

Nolie's expression didn't change. How, then, did he know that a wave of revulsion went through her?

"Thank you, Siobhan, but I can't. I—" She seemed to struggle for an excuse. "I have something else I have to do in the morning."

"Another time, then."

He followed her out to her van and tossed his bag in the back. As soon as they'd started, he looked at her.

"Atheist? Agnostic?"

She shot him an annoyed look. "I'm a Christian. I just don't want to go to church with your family. Is that blunt enough for you?"

"Pretty much." He didn't have the right to ask her

why. She'd confided in him once, and he'd run like a deer. She wouldn't make that mistake again. "If you turn right on Sycamore, that will take us toward the apartment. It's not much out of your way."

They drove a few blocks in an uncomfortable silence. Then she glanced at him.

"What was that business with your brother?"

"What business?" She couldn't possibly know he was worried about Ryan.

"It sounded to me as if you really meant it when you told him to be careful. And it sounded as if he blew you off."

Okay, she did know. Apparently he was more transparent than he'd thought.

"Ryan's young. Cocky. Maybe a little reckless." He moved restlessly in his seat, wishing he could get out and do something. Anything. "I should be there to keep an eye on him."

"Won't Seth and your father do that?"

He shrugged. "He doesn't listen to Seth. They're too close in age, I guess." He wouldn't tell her what Dad's reaction had been. That would just reinforce her opinion. "I've always looked out for the younger ones."

He suspected she understood what he didn't say about his father.

"Have you talked to your mother about it? She seems to have influence over Ryan."

"No. We don't talk to Mom about things that would make her worry." That had always been an unwritten law in the Flanagan household.

Nolie's eyebrows lifted. "You think she couldn't handle it?"

"Look, we just don't." Annoyance sharpened his tone. "You don't know anything about it."

"About mothers?" She tossed the words at him. "Maybe you're right. I don't."

He'd hurt her. He addressed a few unprintable adjectives to himself silently.

"I'm sorry. I didn't mean that."

"Yes, you did." She jerked a nod toward the block of apartments coming up on the right. "You want to tell me where to turn?"

"The second street." He ought to try again to apologize, but what more could he say?

The truth was that he had to find a way to keep some barricades in place between him and Nolie. If she were angry with him—well, that just might work. Because nothing else seemed to.

Nolie glanced around the apartment's living room while Gabe searched for something he wanted in the bedroom. Typical Spartan bachelor fare, as far as she could tell. Gabe had a wall full of CDs, a bank of electronic equipment, an exercise bike and a rowing machine.

Everything else looked like castoffs from the Flanagan house—a sofa with faded slipcovers, a rug with a worn place at one edge.

Did criticizing his decor make her feel any better? Not really. She'd told him things about herself that she'd never told anyone but Claire. And he'd turned right around and used it against her.

Well, maybe that wasn't fair. To do him justice, Gabe probably hadn't even been thinking about her past when he'd made that comment about mothers. He was too obsessed with the problem he felt burdened to solve.

She'd never had brothers or sisters, or at least none that she knew about. So she couldn't really understand the responsibility he seemed to feel for them. As for his worries about Ryan—

She still thought he was wrong about Siobhan. She suspected the woman was a lot stronger than Gabe gave her credit for. In a family where the husband was so outgoing and dominant, maybe that attitude was understandable.

And maybe she ought to give him a break about what he'd said, as well. After all, the poor man hadn't known what he was getting into when he'd probed into her childhood.

As for that kiss—well, it was definitely better not to go there.

Gabe walked back into the room, carrying a couple of books. He went to the bookshelves, clearly searching, and then pulled down some sort of manual. She glimpsed the title. *Advanced Techniques in Fighting Chemical Fires.* Obviously Gabe intended to make use of his time at the farm to prepare for his return to work.

He glanced at her. His blue shirt made his eyes look even bluer, and she sternly told herself to stop noticing things like that.

"So, what do you think of my place?"

She sought for something complimentary to say. "It seems very—um, utilitarian."

He gave a bark of laughter. "Bland and boring, you mean? I guess it is that. Decorating isn't my forte."

He had that right. "You think?"

Gabe grinned, looking around, as if seeing it through her eyes. "I figured it was past time I had a place of my own, but I never seemed to get around to fixing it up. Just stuck in what I needed." He rested his hand on the exercise bike, as if it were an old friend.

She'd like to bring up the little matter of how the dog would fit in here, but she didn't want to start another quarrel. Or hear him say again that he wasn't going to need the dog. She'd save that discussion for another day.

"As long as it suits you, that's all you need. I'd like a little more color and comfort myself, but—"

"That's a woman for you, always wanting to fancy things up. What's wrong with my color scheme?"

"Beige on beige is not a color scheme," she pointed out. "It's a lack of one."

They were talking like casual acquaintances, and she was grateful. If they could just keep things on a nice, professional basis, having Gabe at the farm would be a lot easier.

He grinned. "You might have a point there. I could turn my sisters loose on the place. They'd have a field day."

No girlfriend, apparently. She'd think a man as attractive as Gabe would have a flock of females willing to take on his decorating chores.

"It couldn't hurt."

"Ouch." He gave the exercise bike another pat. "I think that's it. Maybe we'd better get out before you find something else about my place to insult."

She hesitated. "Do you want to take the exercise bike? There's plenty of room at the cottage."

"What about getting it there?"

"We can throw it in the back of the van. Believe me, I've carried bigger loads than that."

"That'd be great, if you're sure you don't mind." He slapped one palm against his jeans. "Using the bike every day would help me get the strength back in this leg."

"Sure thing." She reached for the bike's handles. "I'll take it."

Gabe was already handing her the books. "You take these. I've got it."

They gripped opposite ends of the exercise bike, frowning at each other.

"Suppose we both carry the bike," she suggested. "It's going to be a two-person job to get around the bend in the stairs. I can come back up for the books."

He clearly didn't want to admit that he needed any help, but finally good sense won out and he nodded. "Okay. But I'll come back for the books."

She let it go. If he was determined to climb those stairs again, it probably wouldn't hurt him.

"All right." She lifted the front of the bike, to discover the thing was heavier than it looked. "Ready?"

Together they maneuvered the exercise bike out into the hallway. Gabe set it down long enough to put his books on the floor and lock the apartment door. Then he hefted his end of the bike. "Let's go."

She'd gotten two steps down when Gabe stopped, frowning. "Maybe I'd better go first."

"I'm fine."

He backed up, pulling her along with him. "I'll take point."

She shifted the weight a little, searching for a better

grip as they started down the stairs again. "Is that firefighter talk?"

He shrugged. "I guess. Or basketball. With five kids around our house, we played a lot of basketball. Terry's got a jump shot you wouldn't believe."

"You're almost to the bend," she pointed out. "Better slow down."

He grinned. "Getting too much for you, Lang?"

"You just hold up your share of it," she retorted. "Watch out for—"

Her foot hit a wrinkle in the stair carpet, and she stumbled. The bike tilted, hitting the wall, and Gabe let go to grab her. They ended up pinned into the corner, the exercise bike between them.

"You okay?" Gabe ran his hand along her arm, spreading heat in its wake.

"Fine." She wasn't breathless. Of course not. "Sorry. My foot caught."

"Either that, or you were looking for an excuse to throw yourself at me."

His tone was light, as if he were determined to put that kiss into its proper perspective. She had to match his casual attitude.

"Believe me, if I wanted to do that, I'd pick a more comfortable place. You're standing on my foot, and the handlebars are in my ribs."

"Sorry." He shifted position, his arm brushing hers in the process.

There was that warmth again. She managed to get her breathing under control.

All right, she could do this. The fact that Gabe seemed ready to treat her as if she were one of his sisters should help.

But it was certainly a good reason to keep those fences up between them. She was definitely attracted to Gabe Flanagan, and she needed all the defenses she could get.

"That wasn't so bad, was it?"

Nolie looked as if she really wanted an honest answer to that question. Gabe held the cottage door, letting Max go inside ahead of them.

He forced a smile. "Not too bad, considering."

Actually, he'd hated every minute of the little shopping excursion Nolie had planned for this afternoon. She'd insisted he take Max along to the market. Insisted he say, when questioned about bringing the dog into the store, that Max was a service dog. It was that or have the dog wear a vest saying "service dog" which seemed even worse.

He'd hated it. But he'd done it, because Nolie wasn't about to back down, and he hadn't had a choice.

Nolie flipped the light switch, bringing the main room of the cottage to life. A greater contrast to his apartment couldn't be imagined.

Everything was color and light. The overstuffed sofa, done in blue with yellow accents, welcomed him to relax with a book. The books were there, too, crowded onto a white-washed bookshelf. The shelves more or less matched the white wooden coffee table that looked as if it had been created from a pair of heavy wooden shutters.

An island separated the living space from an open galley kitchen, where red geraniums bloomed on the windowsills. He set the grocery bag he carried on the counter.

"I know it's uncomfortable to speak out about the service dog at first." Nolie began unpacking the bag. "But it gets easier, believe me."

"You should know."

He kept the edge of anger from his voice by sheer force of will. He would be cooperative, even conciliatory. Because before Nolie went back to the farmhouse this evening, he was going to get a commitment from her to talk to the chief. To convince him that by the time Gabe had finished this training, he'd be ready to go back to work.

He'd messed that up before, rushing the subject before he'd even begun to cooperate in Nolie's program. Now they were at the halfway point, and he had a lot more solid foundation for making his case.

Nolie paused, hand on the countertop. "Admitting that Max is a service dog is an essential part of the process. You have to be prepared for the fact that every business won't be as welcoming as my local market."

"What do you mean?"

"Well, just that this was an easy one. Everyone at the market knows what I do here."

"In other words, it was a set-up." He had to work harder this time to suppress his irritation.

"No, of course it wasn't." Nolie planted her fists on her hips, frowning at him. "I wasn't trying to trick you. I simply thought you ought to have an easy experience for your first time out with the dog."

He counted to ten. He would not tell her again that

he didn't need the dog. All that did was raise her hackles, and he wanted cooperation, not a fight.

"Well, it was that." He nodded to Max, who was watching the unpacking process attentively. "Do you suppose he knows I have dog food in this bag?"

Her face relaxed in a smile. "That's a sure thing." She bent, opening one of the lower cabinets, and took out a red plastic dog dish. "Why don't you give Max his first meal in his new home?"

He took the dish, his hand brushing hers, and suppressed the desire to let his hand linger on hers. "What do you think, Max?" He held up the dish. "Dinner?"

Max gave a short bark, as if answering in the affirmative, and his tail wagged.

"Guess that's a yes." He ripped open the bag of kibbles, poured them out, and set the bowl on the white tile floor of the kitchen. Max dug in.

Nolie put a quart of milk in the refrigerator. "I know your mother sent some food along for you, too, but if you've forgotten anything you need, just ask. My kitchen's pretty well stocked."

"Will do." He folded the bag and stowed it under the sink. "The cottage is great. Did you do all this yourself?" It wasn't just a means of getting her on his side. He wanted to know.

She nodded, glancing around the room with a look of satisfaction. "I loved doing it. This place was a tumbledown wreck when my aunt was alive."

She moved back into the living-room area. He couldn't let her get away until he'd brought up the crucial subject. He held up the two-liter bottle of cola he'd bought.

"Can I interest you in something to drink? We can

toast the success of our project." She wouldn't refuse that, and she didn't need to know that the success he had in mind was something different from her vision.

If that was surprise in her face, she masked it quickly. "Sounds good." She sat on the sofa, pulling one of the patchwork cushions behind her.

He dropped ice in glasses, poured, and carried them to the living area, settling next to her on the sofa. He raised his glass to clink against hers. "To success."

"Success," she echoed.

He leaned back. "I'd have to say, this place is a lot more comfortable than my apartment."

"Possibly because I *did* put a little work into it."

"Tumbledown or not, at least your aunt left it to you."

Her lashes swept down, hiding her eyes, and he knew he'd said something wrong.

"Not exactly." She shrugged, staring at her glass as if fascinated by ice cubes floating in cola. "It seems my great-great-uncle didn't entirely rely on her good judgment when it came to property." She gave a faint smile. "By all accounts, he was a typically thrifty German farmer who held on to his land with both hands. Knowing the value of farmland in the Suffolk to Lancaster area, he left it in trust."

It was another little piece to the puzzle of who Nolie Lang was. "Did he think she'd sell the farm and run off to Atlantic City with the proceeds?"

"No." Her mouth clamped shut on the word, and he sensed something repressed with an effort. "She'd probably have given it away."

Something told him not to ask what she meant by that.

"Well, you've done a great job with the decorating, anyway. You must have a gift. Sure you wouldn't like to take on my place?"

She managed a smile. "I'm afraid that might be beyond even my abilities."

He could only be relieved that they'd gotten back onto safe ground. "So, I guess I can expect to do a lot more shopping with you and Max during the next two weeks."

"Among other things. I want you and Max to feel at ease with each other in any situation. I can't duplicate everything you'll run into in real life, but I'll do my best."

"Sounds like fun." Two weeks in close contact with Nolie, as well as Max. He'd be better off if he could go back to thinking of her as plain.

"I do want you to continue working with Danny as much as possible." She gave him a look that seemed a bit wary. "You're good for him, you know. He admires you."

He didn't deserve any admiration. "Kids think firefighters are heroes. We're just people doing a job."

"Plenty of people who aren't kids think the same."

He shrugged, not wanting to respond.

The wariness in her face increased. "Danny really would love a chance to visit the fire station with you."

No wonder she felt wary. Tension surged along his nerves and tightened every muscle. He wanted to slam the subject closed in her face.

But if he were able to open up to Nolie, just a little, this might work to his advantage. It could help move her to do what he wanted.

He took a breath, forcing taut muscles to relax. "I

know he wants to. I wish I could say I'd take him, but I can't. I can't go back as a visitor. I can't go back unless it's for real.''

''I understand how you feel, but—''

He swung his body to face her, reaching out to grasp her hand. ''No, you don't. Don't you get it, Nolie? I have to have the hope of going back to hang on to. I have to.''

Nolie's lips trembled slightly, and her hand turned to clasp his. Maybe she knew that the passion in his voice was real. ''I know. I understand.''

His fingers tightened on hers as if to compel her agreement. Now was the moment. ''If you understand, you'll do something for me.''

''What?'' Caution battled empathy in her voice.

''When I've finished the training, I want you to talk to the chief for me. Persuade him that I've done everything he asked, and I'm ready to go back to work. Please, Nolie. That's not too much to ask, is it?''

''I'm not a doctor. I can't give a medical judgment.'' Her eyes were troubled.

''I'm not asking for that. But he'll be impressed by your opinion.''

He watched her expressive face, reading her inner battle clearly. She wanted to help him. She wouldn't do anything that might endanger her program.

''Please, Nolie. It might make all the difference.'' His fingers caressed hers.

''All right,'' she said finally. ''If you haven't had any seizures by the time your training ends, I'll talk to the chief for you.''

He clasped both her hands in his. ''Thanks. You won't regret it.''

Her eyes darkened. "I hope not."

He was getting her on his side. That could only work to his advantage.

And he wasn't manipulating her, not at all. He was only asking for the truth. The fact that he'd cut down on his seizure medication wasn't her concern. She'd already said she wasn't capable of giving a medical opinion, so she didn't need to know that.

He was right. So why did he feel like such a jerk?

Chapter Seven

"He's impossible."

"Sounds as if he's pretty possible to me." Claire's chuckle floated over the phone line. "Come on, Nolie, loosen up. You haven't been interested in a man in ages."

Nolie frowned at the receiver. "I'm not interested in him. Not as a man, anyway. Just as a client."

"That doesn't eliminate other possibilities." Claire seemed determined to be provoking.

"I'm worried about his suitability as a test case for the foundation, nothing more." She tried to make that sound convincing.

"Well, let's assume that's true, for the moment." Claire didn't sound as though she believed her. "What's wrong with him as a test case? Isn't he co-operating?"

"He'd say he is. But I feel as if he's holding back all the time." Even the evening before, when they'd seemed so close for those few minutes, she'd sensed that. "I think he still actually believes that he's never going to have another seizure."

"You don't agree."

"For his sake, I hope it's true, but what that would do to my case for the foundation, I just don't know."

She rubbed her forehead. She hadn't even told Claire how close that last tax bill had come to wiping her out.

"Well, it wouldn't be your fault if the test case they insisted on turned out not to need a service animal." Claire was practical as always. "Speaking of the foundation, did you decide yet what you're wearing to the foundation dinner?"

"I don't have anything suitable, so there's no deciding to do."

She massaged her temples again, hating the very thought of dressing up for the no-doubt-elegant yearly charitable dinner the foundation put on. Still, as a potential recipient, she couldn't very well have turned down the invitation.

"Not the navy suit," Claire said firmly. "Did you tell Gabe yet?"

"No."

She should have told him that he and Max were expected at the dinner, as well, but she kept taking the coward's way out and avoiding it. He hadn't even wanted to go into the grocery store. How was he going to feel about a fancy dinner?

"Don't put it off," Claire advised.

"That's easy for you to say. You don't have to deal with his reaction."

"You're not letting that man intimidate you, are you?" Claire never let anyone intimidate her.

But she wasn't Claire. "He has a frown that would stop a charging bull."

"Charging or not, tell him. Otherwise you'll just stew about it. Is he there now?"

"No. He went to church with his family."

Thank goodness. Otherwise Claire would be insisting she do it this very minute, while she waited on the phone to be sure Nolie had.

"That sort, are they?" Claire's tone made her opinion clear.

"So am I," she reminded Claire gently. "I just don't do my worshipping in a church."

And Claire didn't worship anywhere. Bringing that up could only lead to a quarrel, and she'd decided a long time ago that quarreling about it wouldn't bring Claire to God. Praying was the only thing she could do.

"Sorry." Claire voice had softened. "I didn't mean anything by that crack."

"I know."

God would reach out and grab Claire one day, she was sure. Until then, Nolie would go on with her quiet witness.

"Anyway, about the outfit for the dinner." Claire's voice regained its usual briskness. "Don't do anything. I'll come out later in the week and bring something."

"You don't have to."

"Yes, I do. You'd probably get the evening equivalent of that navy blazer. And tell the man, for goodness' sake."

"I will." She just wasn't promising when. "I'll see you in a couple of days, then."

Nolie hung up and frowned at the telephone. Anything Claire brought for her to wear was probably going to be far too daring for Nolie's taste, but that wasn't her main problem. Gabe was definitely a bigger issue.

However, she had something much more important to do now. Picking up her Bible, she hurried outside before the phone could ring again. She whistled to the dogs and started down the path that led through the old orchard to the stream.

Gabe had gone to church with his family. With Lady and Max at her heels, she headed for her place of worship.

The Macintosh apple trees that arched over the path, creating an aisle into her sanctuary, had probably been planted by her great-great-uncle. They might be elderly, but their fragrant blossoms still perfumed the air in a scent better than any hothouse lilies.

The stream gurgled and gushed, bank-full after the spring rains. Her feet took the stepping stones with the ease of long practice until she reached the large flat rock that had become her pew.

She sat down, feeling the sun's warmth reflected from the rock beneath her. The dogs nosed along the shallow water at the edge of the creek, intent on business of their own. She was at peace.

She put the Bible on her lap, and it fell open to the verse that had guided her faltering steps into faith. "Now with confidence approach the throne of grace—"

Thank you, Father, for guiding me into Your presence. You know the problem that troubles my heart.

She might not know what to do about Gabe, but Someone did. She could have confidence in that.

"Thanks for the ride." Gabe shut the car door on his mother's repeated invitations to come back to the house for dinner. "I'll see you in a few days."

His father, less interested in what Gabe was having for dinner than his mother, gunned the engine, and the car accelerated back up the lane.

The Flanagans would have to gather around the dinner table without him today. He had business with Nolie that couldn't wait.

He stalked toward the house. Nolie should have realized that in spite of its size, Suffolk was really a small town at heart. Someone was bound to spill the beans about almost anything a person wanted kept quiet.

In this case, the someone had been one of Brendan's parishioners, a wealthy businessman who'd rarely, if ever, bothered to greet the Flanagans after service. And the anything had been the unwelcome news that he and Nolie were expected, dog in tow, at the fancy charity bash the foundation was hosting on Friday.

How long had she intended to wait before she told him? He knocked at the kitchen screen door and then knocked again, more loudly.

No one answered. He peered into the kitchen. "Nolie?"

Nothing. She couldn't be far away. She wouldn't leave the farm with the door to the house standing unlocked.

He stood for a moment on the edge of the porch, looking around. She had to be here someplace, and when he found her, he was going to tell her just what she could do with that charity dinner.

The farmyard lay motionless and quiet in the May sunshine. Not even the usually busy chickens made any noise. The place looked for all the world like an old engraving—''Pennsylvania Farm, circa 1910.''

Then he caught a splash of color and a flicker of movement from the corner of his eye. The movement turned out to be the dogs, chasing each other in the stream. And the bright blue had to be the shirt he'd seen Nolie wear.

He jogged down the steps and crossed the lawn. He had a few choice words to spend on Nolie Lang.

His rapid pace took him through the straggly remains of an orchard, its clouds of white blossoms disguising the gnarled shapes of the old trees. Eyes fixed on Nolie, he headed for the stream.

As he got close enough to see her more clearly, his steps slowed. Nolie sat on a flat gray rock, the stream's water chuckling around it. Her jeans were faded almost to the color of the stone, but the bright shirt probably made her changeable eyes look the same bright blue. Her head was bent, her fair hair loose and flowing across her shoulders.

Something about her stillness made him pause. Nolie looked more peaceful than he'd ever seen her.

Then he realized what she held on her lap. A Bible. Her head was bent because she was praying.

He halted. The sight didn't alleviate his anger, but it did put a check on it. He had to confront her, but not right at this moment. He'd wait until she came back to the house.

He took a step backwards, and a twig snapped beneath his foot. Max's head came up at the sound. Then, with a welcoming bark, the dog galloped toward him.

Nolie's head moved almost as fast as the dog. She'd seen him. There was no point in going back now.

"Hi." He hesitated on the bank. Max plunged into the creek, sending up a spray of water that dampened his gray flannels. "I didn't mean to interrupt you." Well, he had, but not once he saw what she was doing.

"It's fine." She closed the Bible and patted the sun-dappled stone next to her. "Join me. There's something I need to talk with you about."

And vice versa. He stepped from one stone to the next, a little less than sure-footed in his dress shoes.

He reached the rock without incident and lowered himself to sit beside her.

"So this is what you do instead of going to church."

She put the Bible behind her on the flat rock and linked her hands around her knees. "This is church, as far as I'm concerned."

He glanced around, letting the sun's warmth, the ripple of water, the rustle of leaves in the breeze seep into him. He looked at Nolie. Her face was relaxed, the worry lines erased from around her eyes.

"I see your point. Maybe your church did you more good than mine did me."

Surprise flickered in her eyes. "I thought you liked your cousin's service."

"Just kidding," he said quickly. He'd slipped again, saying more to Nolie than he should. No one needed to know just how far away God had seemed to him since the fire. "So, is this how you worship every Sunday?"

She shrugged, her face tightening a little as if she thought he was being critical. "Well, not if it rains."

She clearly didn't want to discuss her outdoor worship, and that fact just made him more curious. "Was this how your great-aunt worshipped?"

"No." Nolie shot the word at him, her head coming up, hands pressing flat against the rock as if ready to shove herself away from him.

He studied her face. A faint flush touched her cheeks as she seemed to realize how much she'd given away with that instinctive response.

"Obviously whatever she did made a pretty negative impression on you." He didn't ask, just left it open, wondering.

She looked at him for a long moment, and then stared down at the water that lapped against the rock inches from her sneakers. "Aunt Mariah would have described herself as a very religious woman."

"How would you describe her?"

Her hands clenched into fists, her tension so palpable that it seemed to reach across the inches between them and sting his nerves to action.

"I'm not sure you want to know."

"I wouldn't have asked if I didn't want to know."

His mind flickered to the reason he'd come looking for her. That issue could wait. Something more important was happening.

Nolie seemed to force her hands to relax, unclenching each finger until they were all loose. "It was a long time ago. Best forgotten."

He studied her face, sensing that he was close to

getting past the barriers she put up. Not sure he wanted to, but somehow compelled to go on.

"You know most of what there is to know about my family. Why so secretive about yours?"

"That's different." She said the words quickly, lashes dropping to screen her eyes. "You're a client. I need to know in order to help you."

A tiny flicker of anger surprised him. "Are you sure that's not just a way of keeping yourself superior? You get to look at me like a dog you're considering adopting, but the dog doesn't have the same right."

Answering anger flamed in her face. "That's ridiculous. I don't do any such thing. You can't possibly compare my aunt to your family—"

She stopped, grimacing as if the words tasted bitter. She wrapped her arms around herself, curling into a protective ball.

He was going on instinct now, not sure what to do, but knowing he couldn't walk away. Couldn't let her keep hiding something that hurt so much.

"Family's family," he said. "Your aunt—"

"My aunt belonged to a cult." She spat out the words. "I don't think your family qualifies as that crazy, do you?"

"Maybe not." Some of the pain seemed to have come out of her on the words. "A real cult, like those people who hang out in airports and beg?"

She shrugged. "Brother Joshua tried to dress it up in Christian terms, but that's what it was."

"Brother Joshua?"

"The leader of the so-called movement. Not that it ever really was a movement. He wasn't charismatic enough for hordes of people to give up everything and follow him. Just a few angry, bitter souls like my aunt.''

He was feeling his way, wanting her to keep talking so that he could understand. ''This Brother Joshua was active around here, was he?''

She nodded. ''He took over a small country church whose parishioners had pretty much died out. He didn't buy it, you understand. Just took it. Said the Lord would want him to have it for his work. That's how he was about everything. Took what he wanted from those who were too gullible to know what they were doing.''

He remembered what she'd said about her great-uncle putting the property in trust. ''That's what you meant when you said your aunt would have given the farm away if she could.''

''She'd have handed everything she owned over to that man.'' Her face twisted, but her words were even. ''She took his word for every little aspect of our lives.''

''Your life, too.''

Nolie's parents had abandoned her. Now it appeared that the refuge she'd found hadn't been a refuge at all.

''Oh, yes.'' Nolie took a deep breath, as if she needed more oxygen. ''Brother Joshua had plenty of opinions on how to raise a child. Most of them involved punishment. 'Spare the rod and spoil the child' was his favorite scripture verse. It was probably the only one he knew.''

For a moment he couldn't speak. Nolie's matter-of-fact tone didn't hide the pain underneath.

''They mistreated you.''

She shrugged. ''Any sane person would call it child

abuse, but there weren't any people you'd call really sane in Brother Joshua's little flock.'' She rubbed her arms, as if just thinking about it chilled her. ''I don't know why I'm talking about it. I don't, as a rule. It's in the past. I survived.''

''You're talking because I goaded you into it.'' Amazing, that he could keep his voice so calm when he was raging inside about what had been done to her. ''How long did it last? Didn't anyone from the outside ever interfere?''

''Brother Joshua was good at claiming freedom of religion when anyone tried to look too closely at his practices.'' She answered the second question first. ''I ran away when I was sixteen. The authorities caught up with me eventually, but by the time they did, my aunt had died.''

She clasped her hands around her knees, rocking back and forth slightly. ''Terrible, to have been glad about something like that, but all I could think was that no one would punish me again.''

He was pressing his hands against the rock so hard they'd grown numb. ''What happened to Brother Joshua? Is it too much to hope he ended up in jail?''

She bent her head, her pale gold hair falling down to shield her face from his gaze. ''I hope he eventually ended up somewhere a lot hotter than that. He faded out pretty quickly once he learned that the inheritance my aunt had promised him consisted only of her personal property. The land came to me.''

''I'm glad you got that, at least.''

She shrugged. ''As I said, it's over. I'm okay.''

Somehow he doubted that anyone who had gone through that could end up being completely okay. He wanted to touch her, to offer some comfort, but she was like a porcupine with its spines out. He touched the Bible instead.

"I'm amazed that you're able to believe after an experience like that."

"That's what Claire always says, too, only in stronger terms." She raised her face, smiling slightly, as if thinking of her friend brought her happiness. "The Bible was the only book my aunt allowed in the house, so I read it out of desperation. And I found a God Brother Joshua had never known—a God who offers unconditional love and mercy."

His throat was almost too tight to speak, but he forced the words out. "I'm glad you found that comfort."

She looked at him then, her face very serious. "I appreciated your mother's invitation, but I don't go to church. That cuts a little too close to the bad memories. I find God here."

"Here." He glanced around. Certainly this was a peaceful spot, but he couldn't imagine staying at the place where she'd seen so much pain. "I'd have expected you to sell as fast as possible and get out."

"Maybe I'm a throwback to that great-great-uncle of mine." Her smile was less strained, as if telling her story had relieved that painful pressure inside her. "I love the land and the animals. They never let me down. I feel as if I've done good work here."

She'd created happiness out of tragedy. Not many people could say that.

"Yes." His voice was husky. "I'd say you've done very good work here."

She turned toward him. ''I shouldn't have unloaded all that on you.''

''I'm glad you did.'' He was surprised to discover that was true.

''That really wasn't what I wanted to talk to you about.''

''What was?'' He suspected she needed to move to some more mundane subject in order to regain her composure.

''Well, the thing is, there's a charity event the foundation is sponsoring on Friday. I'd love to get out of it, but I don't have any choice about going, and I'm afraid they want you and Max to be there, too.''

She looked ridiculously apprehensive at the thought of his reaction. Somehow the complaint he'd intended to make about the foundation dinner seemed petty in comparison.

''Doesn't sound like much fun.''

''No, it doesn't. But you'll go, won't you?''

Maybe, a few hours ago, he could have said no. But not after everything she'd told him today. He couldn't add to her troubles. He was stuck. They both were.

''Good work, Danny.'' Nolie called out the words, focusing on the boy instead of on the man who stood next to Danny as he and Lady negotiated the ramp outside the house. Since she'd been so foolish as to spill her secrets to Gabe the day before, she'd had trouble looking at him.

Danny obviously had no such problem. He grinned up at Gabe in triumph.

She understood why Danny opened up to Gabe. He'd found an object of hero-worship in the firefighter.

She didn't understand her own tendency to open up to the man, though. Gabe seemed able to tap into her deepest feelings. She'd told him things she'd never told anyone but Claire, and that only in the context of the support group in which they'd met.

Gabe was bending over Danny, his face relaxed and teasing as he talked to the boy. Her breath seemed to catch. It was a good thing he didn't look at her that way.

Still, in spite of her discomfort, maybe opening up to Gabe had been a good thing. She hadn't yet found the key to unlocking the inner feelings that kept him from committing to the program. Perhaps eventually her candor would push him into a similar confidence.

"Good job, guys." She walked toward them. "I don't think ramps are going to be a problem for you anymore, Danny."

Danny grinned. "Gabe's got it easy. He doesn't have to figure out how to put on the brakes."

Gabe ruffled his hair. "I'll never be as good as you are, champ."

"Danny and Lady have been working on it for a long time. Maybe when you and Max have been together awhile longer, you'll catch up."

"Maybe." Gabe's eyes darkened, and his tone was noncommittal.

Still, she knew what he was thinking. What he always thought. *I don't need a dog. I'm not going to have any more seizures.*

He could be right, of course. She did a mental count. It had been about a month since he'd had a seizure. His meds seemed to be doing their job, and without any visible side effects. Gabe could be out of the woods.

In which case—

Danny's head turned toward her slightly, his eyes wide and unfocused. His expression sent her heart into overdrive, and a prayer formed automatically in her mind.

Be with him, Lord. Help this child of Yours.

She started toward Danny, but she wasn't fast enough to cover the few feet between them before it happened. Danny lurched backward in the wheelchair, as if yanked by an invisible hand. Before she could reach him, he'd toppled from the chair, his frail body locking in spasms.

Her mind seemed to register several different things as she dropped on her knees next to Danny in the grass.

Lady, moving faster than Nolie had, wedged herself between Danny and the chair, using her body as a buffer so that Danny's spasms couldn't slam him against its metal frame. And Gabe seemed frozen in place.

"Easy, Danny, easy."

She kept her voice calm and soothing. Danny didn't need people around him overreacting when his own brain was misfiring, sending signals his body couldn't deal with. "You're going to be fine. I'm right here with you, and so is Lady."

The dog, hearing her name, whined a little, edging her warm body closer to Danny.

"See." She stroked his forehead. "Lady wants to help. She loves you. We all do." She couldn't let her voice betray the pain she felt for him, no matter how much her heart hurt. Danny needed comfort and strength from those around him now, not pity.

He could use some assurance from Gabe, too. She looked up at him, opening her mouth to tell him so.

She closed it again. Gabe really was frozen. He stood rigidly, fists pressing into his sides. His face expressed shock, maybe horror.

"Gabe!" She deliberately made her voice sharp. Of course it was scary the first time you saw a child having a seizure, but you learned to deal with it. "Snap out of it. I need your help."

She saw the change come over him, as if he turned into the take-charge, in-control firefighter in front of her. His jaw hardened.

"Right. What can I do?"

"You'll find a blanket in the painted chest just inside the kitchen door. Bring it to me. And a tea towel from under the sink."

"Don't you want me to call 911?"

"That's not necessary." Danny's spasms had already slowed, becoming less violent. "He's been through this before. His mother knows how to cope with the aftermath."

He nodded, running toward the house and taking the steps in a single stride. The door banged behind him.

She held Danny closer as the painful rigidity of his muscles began to ease, hoping the warmth of her embrace comforted him.

Unfortunately, she wasn't sure how to comfort Gabe. That look on his face when he'd seen what was happening to Danny had been revealing. He'd been horrified. He'd seen himself.

If he couldn't cope with Danny's seizures, how on earth was he going to cope with his own?

Chapter Eight

"Max, I was just plain stupid." Gabe looked down at the dog.

Max's tail thumped against the wide planks of the cottage floor, and he gave Gabe a doggy grin that suggested maybe his transgression hadn't been too bad.

"You don't need to look so happy. I know how badly I behaved." And how much of an idiot was he, to be confessing to a dog? He ought to be apologizing to Danny.

He seemed to see the boy writhing on the ground again, and his stomach lurched. He stalked to the window and stared out at the rain, trying to erase that image of Danny's seizure the previous day.

It didn't help. He'd relived those few moments all night, feeling again the horror he'd felt when the child he was joking with had suddenly lost all control.

He hadn't caught the boy, hadn't taken control, hadn't done anything but stand there like a stick.

"Even Lady did a better job than I did."

Max waved his tail in agreement.

He was a firefighter, trained to deal coolly with all sorts of emergencies. How could that training have deserted him?

He put his palm on the rain-streaked windowpane, cool to the touch. Danny's mother had just pulled her van up close to the door of the training center, presumably to avoid the wet grass. Danny had reported for his session today as if nothing had happened.

And he hadn't. He hadn't been able to face the kid with the knowledge of his failure fresh in his mind.

Danny's mother emerged from the training center, a black umbrella in her hand. She held it over the chair while Nolie helped load Danny into the van. He could see the boy's hand moving as he waved goodbye to Nolie.

Danny had probably wondered where he was today. Or maybe not. Maybe his behavior had finally disabused the kid of his notion that Gabe was some sort of hero.

The van pulled out. Nolie gave a last wave, turned, and stalked toward the cottage. Her militant stride left no doubt in his mind as to her purpose. He was about to be reamed out, it appeared.

He opened the door as Nolie reached the stoop. She hadn't bothered with a jacket or umbrella, and her T-shirt was spotted with water. Her loose hair clung damply to her neck and shoulders.

She probably wasn't cold. The fire in her eyes would be enough to keep her warm.

All right, he knew he was in the wrong. But that didn't mean Nolie had the right to criticize him.

"You're wet. Come and dry off."

She stepped inside, bringing a breath of rain-swept spring air in with her. "You didn't come for the session with Danny. Why?"

"I usually admire bluntness, but don't you think you're carrying it to an extreme?"

"No, I don't." Her face was uncompromising. "You let Danny down when you didn't come."

Nolie was an expert in how people let children down. The thought stuck like a burr, in spite of his efforts to dislodge it.

None of the excuses he'd been experimenting with seemed worth the effort. Nolie would sweep them aside anyway.

"I let Danny down *yesterday*." He forced the words out. At least they were honest. "I should think he'd have been happy not to see me today."

She looked as if she had measured him and found him lacking. "Danny didn't expect you to behave like a nurse yesterday. He knows people sometimes don't know what to do when he has a seizure."

"He was certainly right about that." He turned away from the laserlike quality of her gaze. "But I should have known. Firefighters are trained to behave appropriately in emergencies."

"You weren't expecting it." Nolie's voice gentled slightly. "There's a difference between behaving appropriately on the job and confronting an emergency with a child you've begun to care for."

"You didn't let that stop you."

"I've had some practice."

Yes, she had. Nolie might not face blazing buildings, but her work still required courage. He managed to look at her again.

"How is he today?"

"Tired." Some of the anger seemed to go out of her at his expression of concern for the boy. "His mother said he slept a lot after the episode. That's normal. But he was ready to go again today."

"He's a brave little guy." *Braver than you are, Flanagan.*

Nolie gave a slight smile, face softening. "His mother sets a good example for him. It's a shame his father hasn't figured out how to face the truth about Danny's condition."

He caught the implication. "I'm not remotely like Danny's father."

"Danny's father lets him down when he refuses to accept the boy's condition. You let him down when you didn't show up today." Whatever softening had been there vanished. "You hurt him."

"Look, I didn't mean—"

No use. He didn't have an explanation that worked for this.

"Never mind what you meant or didn't mean. It's time to face the truth about this." Nolie's expression was uncompromising.

"I am." But even he didn't believe that.

I do good work here, Nolie had said. That was her response to the tragic circumstances of her life. She wasn't expecting anything more from him than she did from herself.

"No, you're not." There was understanding in her face, but she still wouldn't let him off the hook. "You're not facing the real reason you couldn't help yesterday. It's the same reason you didn't show up today. When Danny had his seizure, you didn't see him. You saw yourself.''

''No.'' He rejected it automatically, even as his conscience forced him to acknowledge the truth that Nolie saw.

''Yes.'' She planted her fists on her hips. ''You saw yourself writhing on the ground, out of control, at the mercy of the nerves misfiring in your brain. And you couldn't take it.''

The words stung, but only because they were true. He didn't have anything to say in his defense. There was no defense.

''You will show up for Danny's session tomorrow. You will behave normally toward that child.'' Nolie shot the directives at him.

She didn't wait for an answer. She spun on her heel and stalked to the door, then paused, looking at him with what might have been pity.

''You can be ashamed of your seizures if you want to, Gabe. I can't stop you. But I won't let you make Danny ashamed.''

She walked back out into the rain.

Gabe stared after her, face to face with the unpalatable truth. Nolie was right about him. She looked at him and saw right through his excuses to the man he was.

No hero. Just a man who failed to measure up.

Had she been too hard on Gabe? Nolie glanced toward the cottage the next morning as Danny's mother's van pulled in the driveway. The yellow rambler roses around the door had opened fully, apparently encouraged by yesterday's rain. Otherwise there was no sign of life.

Maybe Gabe wasn't coming. Maybe she'd blown it entirely with him.

She'd understood, only too well, what he'd been feeling. He saw himself in Danny, and since he couldn't bring himself to admit he had a problem, he didn't know what to do with that fact. She hadn't wanted to hurt him, but a painful truth was better than a comforting lie.

She waved, arranging a smile on her face as Myra Trent got out of the van onto the gravel drive and started to unload Danny's chair. If Gabe refused to come back to the sessions with Danny, she couldn't force him. She'd just have to carry on as usual, hoping the boy wouldn't let himself be too affected by his hero's actions.

"Hi, there." She leaned over to hug Danny, and was nearly knocked off her balance by Lady. "Look out, Lady." The dog pushed herself between them, licking Danny's face. "Looks like Lady wants to give you a kiss today."

"Yuck." Danny grinned, hugging the big German shepherd. "Dog kisses."

"You can't fool me." Myra ruffled her son's hair. "You love it."

The lines of strain around Myra's eyes were a little deeper today. Nolie let boy and dog go ahead of her toward the training center and hung back with the woman.

"Did you have a bad night?"

"No worse than usual." Myra massaged her temples, making Nolie wonder how much sleep she'd actually gotten. "Jeffrey came over to see Danny, but it didn't go well."

"I'm sorry." She felt helpless in the face of the woman's problems. "I know how hard that can be on Danny."

"He thinks his father is disappointed in him." Myra's attempt at a smile wavered. "And now he's afraid his new friend doesn't like him anymore."

"Myra, of course that's not true. I'm sure Gabe will make it up to Danny. Really." She hoped.

Myra clasped her hand. "I know you're doing your best." She turned toward the van. "I'll be back in an hour."

Nolie sent another glance toward the cottage as she walked into the training center. Nothing. It looked as if her best wasn't quite good enough.

Danny, laughing, was tossing a ball for Lady to fetch. The sight made her smile even as it touched her heart. The bond between the two of them had increased dramatically since the seizure. It was as if boy and dog alike had realized how much they needed each other.

That was what she wanted for Gabe, too. Unfortunately, her talk must have done more harm than good. It looked as if—

"Hey, how about letting us get into the ball game?"

Her heart gave a little lurch at his voice. She glanced toward the doorway. Gabe stood there with Max, his hand resting lightly on the dog's head.

Gabe probably hadn't gotten much sleep the night before, either, judging by the shadows under his eyes. But the smile he gave Danny was warm.

Danny looked at him for a long moment. "You sure you want to?"

Nolie winced inside. Danny was being honest. Could Gabe really cope with that?

Gabe's face tightened, and he kept his focus on the boy as he went to him. He squatted down so that they were face to face.

"Yeah, I want to." His tone was deeper, as if the words took an effort. "But first, I owe you an apology. Listen, buddy, I'm sorry I didn't know what to do when you had that seizure."

"That's okay." Danny's voice lowered to a murmur, and he looked down.

Her heart twisted. That won't do it, Gabe. He know it's more than that.

"No, it's not okay. I'm a firefighter. We're supposed to be able to handle things like that."

If she clenched her hands any tighter, she'd draw blood. You have to be honest with him, Gabe. *Please, Father, make him see that.*

"You didn't come yesterday." Danny's voice was soft but implacable. "I thought you didn't like me anymore 'cause of the seizure."

Gabe took the boy's small hands in his. "That could never happen. We're friends."

Danny shrugged. "Sometimes people don't want to be my friends anymore after I have one. They think I'm weird."

Please, Lord.

The muscles in Gabe's neck worked, as if he was having trouble swallowing. The moment seemed to stretch on forever. Finally he cleared his throat.

"I don't think you're weird, Danny. I know what it's like, because I have seizures, too."

Tears stung her eyes. He'd finally admitted it. She hadn't been able to get him to that point, but Danny had.

"You do?" Danny's eyes were wide. "Nolie said you got hurt in a fire, but I didn't know you got seizures."

"A beam came down on my head." Gabe managed a smile, and she knew how hard that must be. "I guess that's different from why you have seizures, but the result is the same. So, will you be my friend anyway?"

Danny patted his shoulder, his smile breaking through. "I always will. Promise."

Nolie quickly wiped away the tears that spilled onto her cheeks. She couldn't let them see her crying over them. She took a step closer.

"You know, Danny, Gabe still has a lot to learn about working with Max. Since you and Lady are doing so well, I'll bet you can help him."

"What do you say, Danny?" Gabe stood, still holding the boy's hand. "Do we have a deal?"

"Deal." Danny gave him the thumbs-up sign he'd learned from Gabe.

Gabe ruffled his hair. "Good." He glanced from the boy to Nolie. "You know, I was thinking that maybe we could drop by the fire station for a visit. Would you like that?"

"Wow!" The expression on Danny's face was bright enough to light the city. "Could we really?"

"You bet."

Danny couldn't know how much that offer was costing Gabe, but she did, and her heart ached for him.

"Could Nolie go, too?"

"You don't have to—" she began.

But Gabe was already nodding. Apparently, having decided to do this thing, he wanted to do it all the way.

"Sure, Nolie can come, too. We'll ask your mom when she comes back. Maybe we can meet you there this afternoon."

"Wow." Danny seemed to have run out of words. "Wow. Lady, did you hear that?" He wheeled himself toward the two dogs. "We're going to the fire station. With a real firefighter."

Gabe straightened, watching the boy. Nolie moved closer to him. "That was nice of you," she said softly. "I know it won't be easy."

"No." His lips closed on the word. Then he shrugged. "I owed him. It seemed like that was the least thing I could do."

"It's—" She struggled to find the right words. "It's a costly gift."

"You'd do it. If you were in my place."

"I hope so." She tried to think of a sacrifice that would be comparable for herself, but she couldn't.

His hand closed over hers, and a wave of warmth seemed to flood straight to her heart.

"You would. You're a brave person, Nolie. And a tough taskmaster."

It was hard to sound normal when her heart was singing. "I was afraid maybe I'd alienated you entirely."

"You couldn't do that." His voice lowered to a

baritone rumble that set up a vibration deep inside her. "I know I've been fighting you every step of the way. I probably will again. But that doesn't mean I don't admire you."

"I—I don't—" She was stammering, but she couldn't seem to find the right response.

Gabe's fingers tightened on hers. "Just say thank you. That's enough when someone compliments you."

"Thank you." She didn't dare look at him, because she was afraid he might read too much happiness in her eyes.

She'd like to believe that happiness was for the progress Gabe was making. Unfortunately, it seemed to be more for how their relationship was progressing.

That wouldn't do at all, but she didn't have the slightest idea how to undo it.

Gabe's tension increased exponentially with each block closer to the fire station they came. If Nolie was aware of that, she didn't show it. She just frowned slightly as she negotiated afternoon traffic in the city.

Admitting his condition to Danny had been difficult, but some things were right, no matter how hard. Even if he never had another seizure, he'd had to tell Danny. It had been the only way to make up for his failing.

The image of Danny's seizure was burned into his brain. He hadn't remembered anything about his own seizures. Maybe he'd been lucky. He'd been able to convince himself that he'd just passed out. He still didn't know the truth, and maybe he should.

He glanced at Nolie. She would know the answer to the question that haunted him. "Danny's seizure—was that typical?"

She blinked, as if taken aback by the abrupt question. "Typical? Well, I guess you might say that. A very mild seizure might only manifest as dizziness and disorientation. A severe one could last even longer, be more violent. But I'd say Danny's was fairly typical."

"So that's what I looked like."

He wasn't sure why he could be so honest with Nolie, but he could. Maybe she was the only one.

"You can't help how you look when you have a seizure."

If he was fishing for pity, he clearly wasn't going to get it from Nolie.

"Somehow that doesn't make me feel any better."

"Sorry." Nolie glanced at him. "But that's one of those unpleasant truths we sometimes have to live with."

He didn't intend to live with it. He leaned forward, planting one hand against the dashboard.

"The station is in the next block, on the right. You can pull into the parking lot behind the firehouse."

Nolie nodded, frowning as she watched for the turn.

"A couple of the guys from my crew were in the hospital visiting me when I had the first seizure." He didn't know he was going to say that until the words came out. "I found out firsthand what Danny meant about people looking at you as if you're weird."

Nolie pulled into the familiar gravel lot and turned off the motor. For a moment it was very quiet.

She looked at him gravely. "It took courage to offer to bring Danny here. On a couple of counts."

He shook his head. "Not courage. Like I said, just something I had to do to make it up to him."

She nodded toward the van pulling in next to them.

"Judging by the look on Danny's face, I'd say you're going to be successful."

He took a steadying breath and opened the car door. Showtime. That was what Dad always said when the station call came.

It took a couple of minutes to get Danny unloaded and into his wheelchair—a couple of minutes during which he steeled himself for what was to come.

He wasn't worried about how the guys would relate to Danny. It was a foregone conclusion that they'd be kind. That was an unwritten rule. Firefighters didn't disappoint the kids who looked up to them.

No, the tension that knotted his nerves had nothing to do with Danny. It had to do with how the guys looked at him.

Get it over with. He took a deep breath and pushed the door open. They stepped into the huge, echoing garage. Four firefighters, leaning against one of the rigs, looked up at the sound, their conversation breaking off abruptly.

"Hey, look who's here!" Seth was the first to spot him, and he approached with a huge grin. "Good to have you back, buddy."

Danny glanced up at him with a pleased expression. "That's what you call me," he whispered.

"Well, maybe I can call you that, too." Seth squatted next to the wheelchair. "You must be Danny. I'm Seth, Gabe's brother."

Seth, everybody's friend, would of course be the first one to welcome them. As if that had broken the ice, the others came toward them.

"Danny, these are some of the firefighters I work

with." He'd keep this perfectly normal, for Danny's sake and his own. "This is Jake. Dave. And Laura."

Jake Peters and Dave Hanratty had gone through the academy with him. They'd been in the hospital room when he'd had his first seizure. He managed to look at them squarely. If they were made uneasy by his presence, they were hiding it pretty well.

Danny's attention was focused on Laura Bristow. "I didn't know ladies could be firefighters."

Laura grinned. "Sure they can. If you know any girls who are interested in fire fighting, you send them to me, okay?"

With her brown hair pulled back in a braid and her green eyes dancing, Laura looked like a kid herself, but she was a skilled firefighter. She'd proved her worth, just as every recruit had to do.

Just as he'd have to do all over again, when he came back. If he came back.

"I promised Danny a tour of the station." He pushed everything else out of his mind. "What do you say we start upstairs, okay?"

He bent to pick Danny up, but Seth beat him to it. "I've got him."

He bit back a sharp response. Seth was being kind. He didn't mean to imply that Gabe couldn't carry the boy upstairs.

They trooped up the steps. He heard Nolie and Danny's mom carrying on a conversation with Laura as they folded the chair to take it up, but all his attention was on putting one foot in front of another and keeping a smile on his face.

He'd suggested starting upstairs because he thought that would be easier than the engine room, but no place in the station would be free of memories. He had a lifetime of memories here, starting with the visits he knew only from photos of his father proudly carrying his baby son into the station.

Seth lowered the boy into the wheelchair once they reached the top. He wheeled him into the kitchen. "This is the most important room in the firehouse, Danny."

"It is?" Danny looked up to see if he was kidding.

"Sure thing. There's nothing firefighters like better than eating."

"Except cooking," Jake put in.

"Speak for yourself, Peters. I'd rather do anything else than cook," Laura said.

"*We'd* rather you do anything else than cook," Seth retorted.

The familiar banter was reassuring. Some things hadn't changed.

He wheeled the boy's chair over to the long wooden table, scarred from hundreds of meals, many of them interrupted by the alarm. The kitchen was pretty bare bones, but Dave had taped a couple of bright crayon drawings done by his kids on the refrigerator.

"Don't let them fool you, Danny. We're all pretty good cooks. We have to be, because we take care of everything in the firehouse when we're on duty. We cook, we eat, we study and we even sleep here."

"Hey, who's conducting this tour, anyway?" Seth elbowed him out of the way. "I get to show Danny the rest up here."

"Then I get to do the engine room," Dave said.

Gabe stepped back, letting the tour flow on without

his help. Maybe that was better. He was so keyed up that Danny would probably sense it.

Nolie moved unobtrusively to his side as they went from the kitchen to the living area, where some cast-off family-room furniture in a garish plaid was arranged in front of the television.

"It's not too bad being there, is it?" she asked him softly.

He glanced at Danny, his face alight as he leaned forward to ask Seth something. "It's worth it to see that look on his face."

Somehow her hand had linked with his. Hers felt small, but strong and capable in his. "You're a good man, Gabriel Flanagan."

The others started back toward them then. She drew her hand away from his, but her words lingered, warming him. That was something, to have the respect of a woman like Nolie.

They finished the upstairs, including a snack of Seth's cookies and a display of pole sliding by Laura. Then they trooped back downstairs to view the rigs.

This wasn't hurting as much as he'd thought it would. The guys' attitude toward him seemed pretty normal, although he'd caught Dave eyeing him warily once or twice.

He'd get back on the job soon. They'd see, once he'd been around for a week or two, that nothing bad was going to happen. That they could rely on him.

That was the crux of the matter. No one wanted to be backed up by a firefighter who couldn't do the job. Their lives depended on it.

He wouldn't have a seizure on duty, ever. The job was too important for that. Sure, the work was stressful, but it was good stress, the kind that let him do the job he'd prepared all his life for.

Dave was doing his usual polished tour of the engines. With kids of his own, he knew how to relate, never using words or concepts that were too big for his young audience. It ended, as Dave's tours always did, with Danny wearing a bunker coat and helmet, perched behind the wheel of the rig.

Danny's mother snapped picture after picture. If the boy's grin got any bigger, his face would split.

He could feel Nolie's gaze on him. "Looking good, Danny," he called to the boy. He'd show her that he could cope with being here. He'd be back soon, to stay, and the accident would be just a painful memory, to be revisited now and then in bad dreams. All this would be over.

The shrill sound of the alarm pierced the air. Heads came up as the radio crackled, announcing the call.

Seth swung Danny from the rig, depositing him in his chair.

"Sorry, kid. Got to go."

The others were already scrambling into bunker pants and coats, faces intent as they listened to the details of the call. They rolled into action like the well-rehearsed team they were. The three guys who'd been sleeping upstairs were down the pole in less time than it took to tell it.

Gabe's muscles tensed with the instinct to respond in exactly the way he'd responded hundreds of times before. But he couldn't. He had to step back out of the way, just as much a civilian as Danny or Nolie.

Bitterness rose in his throat like gall. They were

going, the truck rolling out onto the apron already, siren wailing to warn passing traffic. He was left behind.

"Come on, Danny." The boy's mother began pushing the chair. "We'll go outside and watch the engine go down the street."

He didn't move. He couldn't.

"I'm sorry." Distress filled Nolie's soft voice.

He swung toward her, pain clutching his throat.

"I have to come back. I have to." He grabbed her hands, feeling the jolt of emotion flooding from him to her and back again, as if they were connected at some elemental level.

"I understand." Her eyes were bright with unshed tears. For him.

His arms tensed as he battled the urge to pull her into his arms. He wouldn't do that again. He couldn't kiss her, couldn't let himself feel anything for her, because whether she wanted to or not, she stood between him and the thing he'd been put on this earth to do.

He let her go slowly, reluctantly. He wouldn't. But he wanted to. Oh, how he wanted to.

Chapter Nine

"Have another biscuit, Nolie." Gabe's mother urged the basket on her.

Shaking her head, Nolie passed the basket to Gabe, who sat next to her at the Flanagan dinner table. Siobhan had insisted they come for dinner after the fire station visit, but of course she hadn't known then that the trip would be interrupted by an alarm. The faraway look in the woman's eyes suggested to Nolie that her thoughts were concentrated on Seth, not the fried chicken and biscuits.

She'd like to ask if anyone had heard from Seth since he'd gone out on the call, but maybe that was something one didn't ask in a fire fighting family.

Be with them, Lord. Keep them safe.

That was probably the same prayer that was in Siobhan's heart right now.

Ryan, across the table, smiled at her as he passed a platter of fried chicken. A charmer, that one. He'd probably gotten away with a lot in life on the basis of that smile.

"Nolie, why didn't you bring the dog along this time?" he asked. "We all want to meet him."

She didn't need to look at Gabe to know he'd tensed. She could feel it as if they were touching, which was a pretty sad commentary on the state of her emotions where Gabe was concerned.

"I thought maybe one Flanagan at a time was enough for Max," she said lightly.

Gabe's father, in his usual seat at the head of the long table, grinned. "You might have a point, Nolie. But at least the hooligans aren't with us tonight."

"Joe Flanagan, don't you call your grandchildren hooligans." Siobhan took mock exception to that. "They aren't nearly as bad as our kids were, as I recall."

"Only because there were more of us, Mom," Terry said.

"Speak for yourself," Gabe said, grinning. "I was the perfect child."

The others hooted at that, and Nolie relaxed, relieved that the conversation had moved so easily from the subject of Max. She could hardly have said that Gabe had flatly refused to have the dog with him on his trip to the fire station.

She'd understood, but that didn't mean she wouldn't have insisted, had it not been for Danny. She hadn't wanted to take the risk of Danny's visit to the fire station being put in jeopardy because the adults couldn't come to a reasonable agreement.

Still, she had to accelerate the pace of Gabe's work with Max. Time was slipping away, and they hadn't done nearly enough teamwork in public places. She couldn't let her sympathy for Gabe interfere with the work they had to do.

Sympathy? The voice of her conscience inquired. Is that what it is?

She didn't think she was ready to answer that question.

Lord, help me with this, please. I don't want to let my feelings for Gabe override my good judgment.

She glanced up to find Gabe's cousin, Brendan, watching her. She looked away quickly, concentrating on cutting up her chicken. It wasn't Brendan's fault that she felt uncomfortable in his presence. He certainly couldn't have known that she was praying, or what that prayer was.

Had Gabe told him about her past? She'd like to believe Gabe wouldn't have talked about what she'd told him, but she honestly didn't know. For that matter, she still didn't know why she'd told him. She didn't normally talk about that to anyone.

If you were really over the past, the way you say you are, you wouldn't mind talking about it.

Her conscience seemed remarkably active today. She told it to be quiet and returned her focus to the dinner-table conversation, which had moved on to an assortment of stories about the Flanagan brood's misadventures when they were kids.

She leaned back, enjoying the tales even without being able to take part. By the sound of it, Ryan and Terry had been the mischief makers, constantly having to be pulled out of trouble by Seth or Gabe.

"What about you, Nolie?" Terry smiled at her.

"Don't you have any hair-raising stories of driving your poor parents crazy when you were a kid?"

Gabe's hand closed over hers under the table. Well, obviously he hadn't told Terry, at least.

"I'm afraid I didn't have any brothers or sisters to lead me into trouble."

"Maybe you were lucky, at that," Ryan said. "There are days when I'd give you some of mine."

"Not a chance." Terry gave him a mock punch. "You can't give us away. Who'd keep you out of trouble? We'll just make Nolie an honorary Flanagan. Then she can have all the pleasure of having a big family with none of the disadvantages."

"How do you figure that?" Brendan asked. "If she's an honorary Flanagan, don't the disadvantages come with it?"

"What disadvantages?" Joe demanded.

She listened with amusement to the argument that arose over whether there actually were any disadvantages. They didn't begin to know how lucky they had it, but she didn't feel even remotely envious. Instead, she almost felt as if she did, indeed, belong.

That was a dangerous thing to start feeling. When her relationship with Gabe ended, her relationship with his family would, too. She glanced down at his hand, still holding hers. She didn't want that to happen. But it would.

She didn't like the hollow feeling that thought produced.

The argument ended with a clatter of dishes as everyone began clearing while Siobahn brought coffee in. The telephone rang. Perhaps no one but Nolie noticed how white Siobhan's fingers were as she set the tray down carefully.

Gabe picked up the receiver, and his face relaxed in a grin as he said Seth's name. After a few joking comments, he hung up.

"Nice, smoky tire fire at that lot out toward the Randallstown road. No injuries, but they'll all smell like burning rubber for a while."

Siobhan's relief came toward Nolie like a wave of emotion.

Thank you, Lord.

She suspected they were both thinking the same thing, but apparently the Flanagan way of dealing with worry was to ignore it or joke about it. That had to wear on a person after awhile, and Siobhan had had years of it.

"Coffee, Nolie?" Gabe's gaze seemed to warn her not to say anything about Seth's call.

"No, thanks." She glanced at her watch. "I hate to eat and run, but the animals have to be fed, too."

He nodded. "I'll wait and have my coffee at the cottage, then. Mom, we're going to head out."

"Just a second." Siobhan fished in the pocket of the loose cardigan she wore. "I nearly forgot to give you these." She handed a prescription vial, filled with orange tablets, to Gabe. "I picked up the refill on your medication. You must be almost out."

Gabe's expression didn't change as he took the vial and slid it into his pocket. "Thanks, Mom."

Nolie said her goodbyes, went down the walk and started the car with a preoccupied mind.

Gabe's medication, his mother had said. His seizure medication, the medicine he should have been almost out of. But she'd seen the bottle on the kitchen counter at the cottage, and it was still more than half full.

She didn't like her conclusion, but it was inescapable. Gabe wasn't taking his seizure meds.

She'd wait until they were clear of town traffic. There was no sense in courting an accident by starting what was undoubtedly going to be a quarrel.

Once they were on the two-lane macadam road that led to the farm, she couldn't hold back any longer.

"You've stopped taking your seizure medication, haven't you?" She gripped the steering wheel as if it were Gabe's shoulders and she was shaking him.

"No." He shot the word back in instant denial, but he didn't look at her.

"Don't kid me, Gabe. I've seen the medication vial at the cottage. Your mother said you should be almost out. You're not."

He had one hand pressed against the dash. If the car hadn't been moving, he'd probably have jumped out. "All right. Not that it's any of your business, but I started cutting down on the medication. It's time I went off it."

"According to whom? Your doctor didn't tell you to do that, did he?"

"If I'm not having seizures, I don't need medication."

She really would like to throttle him. "You may very well not be having seizures because of the medication. Has that thought occurred to you?"

He shook his head stubbornly. "I don't need it. It's time I got back to normal. I can't return to work if I'm taking seizure medication."

She hadn't thought of that. "Are you sure? If the

seizures are under control, it's possible taking the medication wouldn't be a bar to going back to work.''

The stubborn set of his jaw said that he didn't intend to discuss it. ''I don't know. And I don't plan to find out. I'm doing fine on a reduced dose.''

''I see.'' She saw several things, and she didn't like any of them. ''When were you planning to let me in on this?''

His glance gave her the answer to that one. Never.

''You weren't going to tell me, were you?''

A muscle twitched angrily in his jaw as he gritted his teeth. ''You're not responsible for my medical well-being.''

''No. I'm just the one you asked to talk to the fire chief about your readiness to return to work. Remember that?''

''I'm not asking you to lie.''

''No. Just to omit the little fact that you haven't been taking your medication the way you should.''

''Look, if I'm getting along fine taking a lower dose, doesn't that prove I'm ready to go back? I don't need—''

He stopped, but she knew what he'd been going to say. He didn't need her or her program.

He was close enough to her in the car that she could reach out and touch him. But he was farther away than ever. He didn't intend to let her help him, and there was probably nothing she could do about that.

''I've never been here, so I can't vouch for the food.''

Nolie glanced toward him as they approached the

small restaurant in Randallstown the day after they'd visited the station. He tried to muster a smile in return.

"I can eat almost anything for lunch. It'll be fine."

He didn't say what they both knew. That she hadn't wanted to go to a little local place near the farm, where everyone already knew about her work. She'd wanted more of a challenge for this outing with Max. She'd suggested a popular place right in downtown Suffolk. His *no* had been quick and emphatic.

He wasn't going to appear with the dog and a handler in a place where he could very easily run into someone he knew. He looked down at Max, walking sedately at heel. He'd convinced Nolie not to put the vest on the dog. Max might appear to be a pet to any casual observer.

Nothing personal, Max. But you should be with someone who needs you. I don't.

So they'd settled on a restaurant neither of them knew in the nearby town. His relationship with Nolie seemed to be one long compromise.

He held the glass-paned door for her to precede him, and Nolie walked in without a word. She'd been giving him the silent treatment except for necessary instructions since their blowup the night before about his meds.

His irritation still rankled, and he shot a look toward her as they waited for the hostess. Nolie's pale blond hair was loose on her shoulders today, and she'd worn an aqua sweater that made her eyes look more aqua than blue. Days spent in the spring sunshine had brought a glow to her skin that hadn't been there the first time he'd seen her.

He'd thought her plain then. What had been wrong

with his eyes? She was anything but. Her face might be too strong to be called conventionally pretty, but it had a classic look that would last a lot longer than prettiness.

The hostess came hurrying toward them, heels clicking. "Sorry." She flipped her dark bangs, automatically giving him the look she probably gave every presentable man who walked in. "Two for lunch?"

He nodded. "Nonsmoking, please."

She picked up two menus. "This way—" She stopped abruptly halfway around the counter and stared at Max. "You can't bring a dog in here."

He knew what he had to say. Knew, too, that Nolie would stand there as long as necessary until he said it. He gritted his teeth.

"Max is a service dog. He is permitted to accompany me to any public place." He tried to say it with the same assurance Nolie did.

"I don't know." The hostess still looked doubtful.

He took a deep breath in order to force the words out. "You can't legally deny access to a person who relies on a service animal."

Whether it was the legal implication or not, he didn't know, but after a moment she nodded, then led them to a table in the half-filled dining room. He held Nolie's chair for her, and her hair moved like silk against his forearm as she sat down.

He took the seat opposite her, and Max lay down quietly next to him.

"That wasn't so bad, was it?" Nolie's gaze was serious.

"No." He realized he'd clipped the word off and shook his head. "Sorry. I'm just not used to this."

She didn't bother to say the obvious—that getting used to it was the whole purpose of the exercise. Max was probably better prepared than he was.

He picked up the menu and sought for words to ease the situation. "Do I order something for Max?"

"He's working. Max doesn't eat on the job."

Heavy footsteps sounded on the tile floor, drawing his attention. The heavy, balding man who headed toward them wore a chef's apron and a scowl. He rumbled to a halt next to them and glared at Max.

Gabe's tension went up a notch. This wasn't going to be as easy as he'd hoped.

"You can't bring a dog in here." The man's tone didn't allow for argument. "There are tables out on the sidewalk. We'll serve you there."

His impulse was to agree to anything that would get this awkward moment over, but he knew better. And if he didn't, Nolie's look would tell him everything he needed to know.

"Max is a service dog." He kept his voice low. He had no particular desire to advertise to the rest of the restaurant. "You can't deny access to someone with a service dog."

The man's face reddened. "Listen, I don't need you to tell me the law. Law says I have to let people in with seeing-eye dogs, okay, I do it. But you got two good eyes, and I don't want that dog in here."

If Gabe's jaw got any tighter, he wouldn't be able to speak. "People use service dogs for other disabilities besides blindness."

He should say that he required the service of a seizure dog. That was what Nolie expected. He couldn't.

"You don't look disabled." The man's voice rose,

and people at other tables began to stare. "Now take the dog to an outside table or leave. I don't have to serve anybody I don't want to serve."

He felt Nolie's gaze on him, expecting something from him he couldn't give. All he wanted to do was to shove his chair back and walk out. He couldn't do this, and she might as well know it.

"You're wrong."

Apparently she did. Nolie's voice was not loud, but it was as determined as the restaurant owner's.

"You can't deny service to a disabled person, whether that person is accompanied by a service animal or not."

"He doesn't look—"

"Whether or not a person looks disabled is not the point." She swept on, passion filling her tone. "According to the Americans with Disabilities Act, you don't have a choice. Mr. Flanagan is accompanied by a seizure-alert dog. If you refuse to serve us, our next step will be to report that this restaurant is in violation of the law."

On second thought, maybe he'd rather crawl under the table. Anyone in the restaurant who hadn't been looking at them before was looking now. He didn't know whether he was angrier at the lout of an owner or at Nolie for making a scene.

The man glared at them for a second longer. It hung in the balance. Then he turned and lumbered away. At least he was smart enough to know when he was defeated.

Gabe waited until people had returned to their interrupted meals. Until he could trust himself to keep his voice low.

"Did you have to do that?"

Her brows lifted. "Of course."

Of course. He planted his hands on the edge of the table. "Now that you've made your impassioned speech for the day and won, let's get out of here."

"We can't do that." Her expression was sympathetic but unyielding.

"Why not? You've proved your point."

She glanced around, as if to be sure people weren't still watching them, and then leaned across the table to put her hand over his. Her fingers gripped his firmly.

"We can't walk out. If we do, that man will feel as if he's won."

He glared at her. "Do you think I care about that?"

She seemed to withdraw, even though she didn't take her hand away. "You should. Do you want it to be Danny they refuse to serve next?"

He wrested his hand free. "Isn't that hitting below the belt?"

"Not if it makes you realize the responsibility you have when you walk into a restaurant with a service animal. You're representing every other person who relies on one. You can't leave just because it's a little unpleasant."

She wouldn't say the unpleasantness was little if she were the one who had to admit to a disability. Or maybe she would. All he knew was that he couldn't.

"All right." He ground out the words. "I'll stay." He pushed on before the look of relief could take over her face. "But understand this, Nolie. I might not have a choice about being your test case for the foundation, but that doesn't mean I'm going to be a poster boy for your program.''

Her lips compressed. ''I know. You don't think you need Max or the program. You're never going to have a seizure again.''

''That's right. And if it's not—'' He stopped. He didn't want even to admit the possibility, but he had to make her understand how strongly he felt. ''Even if I'm wrong, that doesn't change how I feel. I don't know how I'd deal with it, but I do know I wouldn't go around advertising the fact by working with a dog. I won't do it.''

Gabe had looked at her as if he'd hated her. That memory made Nolie's steps falter as she walked toward the cottage that evening. She clutched the folder she held a little tighter. Maybe he did.

Her practical side swept that thought away. Self-pity is not becoming. Gabe doesn't hate you. He doesn't feel anything for you.

Maybe that was even worse. Still, she couldn't expect anything else. If she and Gabe had met in any other circumstances, they'd have had nothing in common. Because of how they'd met, they had something huge in common, but that something seemed to be an irrevocable barrier between them.

The spring evening air was so soft and misty it was like walking through a cloud perfumed by roses and lilacs. Too bad she was too nervous about what she had to do to enjoy it. She pushed herself toward the cottage.

Her rap on the cottage door sounded peremptory.

Well, good. She'd hold on to any shield between them she could.

Gabe opened the door, Max at his heels.

"Nolie. Hi." His tone was cautious, his gaze a bit wary. Maybe he felt ashamed of his outburst, but if so, he'd never admit it to her.

"I have something for you." She held out the folder, prepared to turn and leave.

He stepped back, motioning her inside. "What is it?"

"A copy of the Americans with Disabilities Act." She moved into the cottage, bracing herself for battle. "I know you don't want it. You don't care about it."

He closed the door. "I didn't say that, exactly. I said it didn't apply to me."

She had to tell him what she'd come to say, not let her gaze dwell on the innate strength of his features or his determined stance.

"Look, even if you're healed, even if you never have another seizure, this is something you should know. If not for your sake, then for the sake of kids like Danny. You can't pretend problems don't exist."

"Not after today, I can't." His face tightened, and she wasn't sure what he was thinking.

"If you're still angry with me—"

He shook his head abruptly. "I'm not. I'm angry with that jerk at the restaurant. You were right. If he'd treat me that way, he'd treat other people that way."

A trickle of relief went through her. At least Gabe seemed to be thinking.

"It happens, more often than it should. Things are better than they used to be, but they're far from perfect."

He put the folder down on the lamp table. "I'll read it. I promise. I'll even make it required reading the next time I teach a training seminar at the station."

"Thank you." Gabe's concession wasn't an admission the Act applied to him, but it was probably the best she'd get. "The fire department could probably use a refresher course."

His face relaxed in a smile, and he leaned his hip against the back of the sofa. Max, apparently deciding nothing interesting was going to happen, flopped down on the rag rug inside the door with a sigh.

"The guys would probably find it a welcome relief from the latest lectures on analyzing building stress or fighting chemical fires."

If he was prepared to talk normally with her, she had to encourage him. "I didn't realize fighting fires was so technical."

"I know. You civilians think all you have to do is point a hose and turn on the water."

"Well, I did know there was a bit more to it than that." Still, she was probably as woefully ignorant of his work as he was of hers.

"Training, training and more training. So when the real thing comes along, you know what to do by instinct." The humor faded gradually from his face. "It has to become instinct. When the alarm goes, you don't know whether you'll be hosing down the highway after a tanker spill or making a grab from a highrise apartment building."

"A grab?"

"Firefighter talk for rescue."

It was the most he'd ever talked to her about his

work. She didn't want him to stop. She wanted to understand.

"Have you done that? Actually rescued someone?"

He shrugged. "A few times. That's probably what every kid dreams of when he thinks of being a firefighter. Rescuing someone from a burning building. It's actually a matter of luck as much as anything. You have to be at the right place at the right time."

"And if you're not—"

"Then someone else does it. But you always want to be in on it. That's what you live for, if you're a firefighter."

That was what Gabe lived for. Her heart overflowed with the longing to give him back what he'd lost.

"I know how much you want to get back to your real life. Believe it or not, that's what I want for you, too." She reached out toward him almost instinctively, and his fingers closed over hers, sending that now-familiar wave of warmth through her.

"Do you, Nolie?" His gaze held hers, searching, as if he were looking into her heart and seeing all the secrets she held there.

"Yes." It was barely more than a whisper. She shouldn't let herself be drawn to him, certainly shouldn't open herself to him. That could only lead to heartbreak, but she couldn't seem to stop. "I understand how important fire fighting is to your family."

"It's not just that." He had both her hands in his now, drawing her inexorably closer. "Sure, the family thing is a big part of my life, but there's something bigger than that. The fire where I was hurt—two of my brother firefighters died in that fire."

She struggled to understand. "You can't feel guilt—"

He shook his head, his fingers tightening on her wrists so that he must feel the pulse that pounded there.

"Not guilt. Anger. Retribution. Fire is the enemy. That day the enemy won. I can't let that happen."

His passion enveloped her, drawing her to him, as helpless as a leaf plucked by the wind. His gaze focused on her face, piercing, heating. She had no defenses left.

His eyelids flickered. His gaze lost focus. Max made a throaty sound and started toward them as her arms went around Gabe in a futile effort to cushion his fall. He was having a seizure.

Chapter Ten

Gabe poured coffee into a mug the next morning, inhaling the rich aroma. It didn't help. All the coffee in the world wasn't enough to wipe the remnants of last night's seizure from his mind or his body.

He shook his head, trying to shake away the paralyzing sensation of the heavy sleep he'd fallen into afterward. His head felt as if it were packed with cotton.

He took a gulp of the coffee. Any feeling, including anger, would be better than this lethargy that seemed to sap his will.

Someone rapped at the door. Even if he hadn't known it had to be Nolie, Max's enthusiastic tailwagging would have identified her.

"Come in." The effort of crossing the room to let her in was too much.

"Good morning." Nolie paused inside the kitchen door, her blue eyes grave as they assessed his condition. "Coffee smells good. Is there an extra cup?"

"Help yourself." He slumped into one of the ladder-back chairs at the small round table in front of the window. "There's milk in the fridge, if you take it."

"Black's fine." She poured coffee and carried a mug over to the table, setting it on the apple-printed placemat before sitting down opposite him. "How are you this morning?"

Max put his head on Nolie's knee with a soft whine, and she patted him.

He shrugged. "Okay. Sleepy."

"That's pretty common, but I guess you know that."

"Yes." Unfortunately, he did. "Aren't you going to say I told you so?"

She ruffled the fur around Max's neck, and the dog fixed her with an adoring gaze. "Why would I do that?"

"Because you warned me not to cut back on the medication." He forced himself to admit it. Fair was fair. "I didn't listen."

"That doesn't give me any pleasure. I wish I'd been wrong." She honestly seemed to mean that.

"Thanks." He took another gulp of the coffee, relieved to notice that his head was starting to clear, maybe just from making the effort to talk. "Well, I'm back on the recommended dosage now, you'll be glad to know."

He hoped that didn't sound bitter, but even bitterness was preferable to struggling through a gray fog, like a dream where you had to run but couldn't.

"That's good." Her voice was carefully neutral. "Danny will be here in about half an hour."

He couldn't. He pressed both palms flat against the

tabletop, trying to come up with a reason she'd accept. Maybe the truth was his only option.

"Nolie, let me off the hook this morning, okay? I just need to clear my head before I see anyone else, even Danny."

She studied his face for a long moment, as if measuring the honesty of his words. Finally she nodded. "All right. You can have the morning off, as long as you don't try to get out of tonight."

Tonight. The foundation event. "I can't—"

"Don't even think about it," she said quickly. "We have to be there tonight. Believe me, I don't like it any better than you do, but neither of us has a choice."

He'd agreed to this. "Right. I'll go. I won't promise to enjoy it, but I'll go."

Her smile sparked. "Well, that will be two of us not enjoying it. In the meantime, I'll let you off working with Danny, but don't sit around the house."

"I thought I'd take a walk in the woods."

He hadn't really thought any such thing, but now that he'd said it, it sounded like a good idea. A little time alone in the fresh air would finish the job of clearing his head.

She nodded, as if she understood his purpose. "You'll find a path behind the barn. It circles around and eventually leads to the top of the hill. Take Max. He knows the way."

"I'll find it."

"Take Max," she repeated. "Please."

His hands tightened around the mug. "You think I'll need his help today, is that it?"

Her expression didn't change at his sharp tone. Maybe she was used to working with irritable clients.

"Probably not, but take him, anyway. He deserves the reward of a walk in the woods. He did everything right last night."

Last night, during the seizure. He'd felt Nolie's arms around him, cushioning his fall. He'd felt Max, too, putting his body between him and the table. Protecting him.

"He didn't know the seizure was coming."

He hadn't intended to say that. What difference did it make, when he had no plans to be dependent on the dog, anyway?

"It's true he didn't alert you." Nolie's brows knitted. "But it was the first seizure you've had since you've been working together. We can't really train for that response. I believe it will happen, given time."

"Given some more seizures, you mean."

"Gabe—" Nolie paused, seeming to edit what she was about to say. He thought that sympathy lurked in her eyes, but she kept her voice matter-of-fact. "I hope you don't have another seizure. I've told you that."

His jaw hardened. Did she actually believe that? How could she separate what was good for him from what was good for her program?

"I thought I was over them."

"Maybe you are. After all, that was a fairly mild one. You never completely lost consciousness."

"I'm not sure that's a good thing." He'd been able to feel the exact moment when his body stopped obeying his commands, betraying him.

"I know." Her hands moved, as if she wanted to reach for him but she restrained herself. "But it is more encouraging than having a severe seizure. And if you'll take your medication the way you should—"

He held up his hand to stop her. "Lesson learned. I promise I'll take it."

But if he did, what were the odds the department doctor would pass him to go back on active duty? He didn't have an answer to that.

She did reach out to him then, clasping his hand in both of hers. "I know you're disappointed. I'm sorry."

He stood abruptly, his chair scraping back. Her hands dropped away from his.

"I don't want to talk about this right now."

Her lashes fell, but not quickly enough to mask the pain in her eyes. He'd hurt her.

She stood, her face once again composed. "I understand. But please take Max with you today."

He'd rejected her sympathy, pushed her away when all she wanted was to help. Still, he couldn't talk about this with her, of all people. She had too much invested in him.

So he'd hurt her.

"I'll take Max with me. I promise."

Now please go away. The message couldn't have been clearer if he'd spoken the words.

"Well, when are you going to tell me about him?" Claire spread the dress she'd brought on Nolie's bed.

Nolie looked at the dress doubtfully. The sophisticated froth of black silk chiffon looked incongruous on the double-wedding-ring quilt that covered the four-poster. If she argued about the dress, maybe Claire would forget about Gabe.

"I really don't think—"

"You don't have to think. If you had any fashion sense, I wouldn't have to do this."

Claire eyed Nolie's faded jeans with disfavor. Even dressed casually for her fashion emergency trip to the farm, Claire radiated elegance.

"Now get rid of the jeans and sneakers so you can try this on."

Arguing with Claire in a makeover mood was like having a discussion with the tornado that was sweeping your house away. Nolie obediently kicked off her sneakers.

"I'm not a foundation patron. I'm a beggar." She suspected this argument wasn't going to go anywhere, but she'd give it a try, just so Claire wouldn't get used to pushing her around. "Maybe I ought to look poor and needy when I meet them."

"This is a social event, even if you are there to conduct business." Claire yanked Nolie's T-shirt out of her hands and tossed it across the room. "Believe me, people like this want to feel as if they're giving their money to someone like them. If you went in looking needy, they'd think you wouldn't know how to handle your grant."

"Maybe." She hadn't gotten that impression from her one encounter with Mr. Henley, but Claire knew more about people like him than she did.

Claire handed her a pair of pantyhose. "Never mind arguing about the pantyhose. I want to see the complete effect of the outfit, pantyhose and all."

Nolie sat down on the birds-eye maple rocker she'd found at a yard sale and painstakingly refinished. "You know I hate these things. I always feel as if they're cutting off my circulation."

"You have to suffer a little, or you're not properly dressed." Claire frowned at her. "Well? When are you going to tell me about him?"

It would do no good to ask who she was talking about. They both knew.

"There's nothing to tell." She eased the black filmy stocking over one leg. "He's a client."

"He's a gorgeous hunk of man."

She could hardly say she hadn't noticed, but she certainly wasn't going to admit the depth of her feelings.

"All right, he is. But we have a professional relationship, that's all."

"The way you looked at him didn't seem too professional to me."

She concentrated on pulling up the pantyhose without snagging them. "You're imagining things. I look at him the same way I look at every client."

"Sure you do. And what about the way he looks at you?"

She couldn't stop her gaze from jumping to Claire's face. "What do you mean? How does he look at me?"

"Like you're a tall glass of cold water after he's been fighting a fire."

"That's certainly not the most romantic thing I've ever heard."

Claire shrugged. "I don't know about that. A man will die without water." Her eyes twinkled. "So you do want romance."

"No, I don't. I keep telling you, we just have a business relationship. Neither of us is looking for anything else."

That speech might have been more impressive had

it not been muffled by the dress Claire was slipping over her head.

"You might not be looking for it, but it found you. Besides, .your professional relationship doesn't preclude a personal one. You won't be his trainer forever."

"It still wouldn't work." Why couldn't Claire leave it alone? "Even if the whole thing with my work and the grant didn't come between us, our family backgrounds are just too different. We'd never find any common ground. We both know that."

Claire paused, the zipper halfway up Nolie's back. "You told him about your childhood?"

Now she'd done it. Claire knew she never talked about her history.

"It just sort of came out one day when we were talking. It doesn't mean anything."

"Sure." Claire ran the zipper up the rest of the way.

"It doesn't."

"You keep telling yourself that, sweetie. Maybe you'll actually start to believe it." She swung Nolie around so that she was facing the full-length mirror. "There. That's the woman the foundation people are going to see tonight."

Nolie blinked. The black dress clung to her body sleekly, and then burst into a flirty ruffle at the hem, drawing the eye to her legs. Claire had swept her hair back from her face to cascade down her back, so that the sparkly earrings she had brought dangled against her neck.

"That's not me."

Claire laughed. "That is definitely you." She gave her a quick hug, enveloping her in a wave of fragrant scent. "The you that's been in hiding. Now don't let the wicked aunt or Brother What's-his-face out of the closet tonight."

"I won't." She hoped.

"And enjoy Gabe's response when he sees you."

"Claire, I keep telling you—"

"And I keep not believing you." Claire waved an airy goodbye. "Enjoy. And don't come home early. Your coach won't turn into a pumpkin, I promise. You can dance with Prince Charming until midnight."

She was gone before Nolie could come up with a suitable retort, even supposing there was one that didn't reveal how much she wanted to have Gabe look at her as if she really were his Cinderella.

Gabe glanced at his watch as he headed back toward the cottage. He had plenty of time to get ready, and thanks to the tramp in the woods, he actually felt human again. Maybe he'd be able to get through being put on display tonight.

As he crossed between the barn and the paddock, he spotted the woman who stood by her car on the lane. Nolie's friend, Claire, looked as if she were waiting for something. Or someone.

He veered from his path and walked over to her. "Hi. I'm Gabe Flanagan. We met a couple of weeks ago."

"I haven't forgotten." Her gaze assessed him. "You're Nolie's prize client."

Something about that measuring look annoyed him. "I don't know about the prize, but I'm one of Nolie's clients, yes."

"More than that, I think." She frowned, and he

realized that was concern in her eyes. Not for him, so it had to be for Nolie. What was bugging the woman?

He shrugged. "Our work is supposed to lead to the grant, so in that sense it's more."

"She told you about her past." Claire gave him an uncompromising frown.

"Yes, she did."

I never tell anyone, Nolie had said. But she'd told him.

"Then you know how vulnerable she is after living through that horror. She could be hurt easily by someone she cared about. I don't want that to happen." The steely look in Claire's eyes suggested she'd know what to do to someone who hurt her friend.

He stiffened at the implied threat. "I appreciate your caring for Nolie, but I'm not sure it's necessary. She's a grown woman. She survived an awful childhood, but she's over it now."

"Over it?" Claire's brows rose until they disappeared behind her auburn bangs.

"Yes." He wanted this conversation finished. The woman didn't need to lecture him about Nolie.

"If you think she's over it, go take a look in the shed behind the barn."

"What are you talking about?"

She ignored his question, swinging into her car. "Just do it. And be careful with her."

She revved the motor and spun out in a spray of gravel.

He looked at Max. "That is one irritating woman."

Max waved his tail.

"Still, I guess it wouldn't hurt to take a look."

As if he agreed, Max fell into step with him. They

strode toward the barn, then past it. The barn's bulk sheltered them from the house. Unless Nolie came outside, she wouldn't see what they were doing.

He glanced, frowning, at the shed. It was a tumbledown affair, its gray unpainted planks a contrast to the well-kept appearance of the rest of the farm outbuildings. He hadn't noticed that before, but now that he did, it stuck to his mind like a burr.

His feet were following a path through the tall grass. So even though the building looked desolate, someone must come here.

Not someone. Nolie. There wasn't anyone else.

He didn't want to go on, but Claire had told him to. Unless he very much missed the mark, Claire cared for Nolie more than anyone. She wouldn't tell him to look in the shed unless there was something there he had to see.

He tugged on the knob. Locked.

Max whined, as if he didn't like this any better than Gabe did.

"I think we have to look, Max. Otherwise we'll always wonder." He reached up to the top of the door frame. Sure enough, his fingertips touched the cold metal of a key.

He pulled it down and slid it into the lock. It turned easily.

"Come on, buddy. We'll go in together."

He shoved the door open, releasing a shaft of light that didn't do much to penetrate the gloom within. He stepped inside, groping automatically along the wall to the right until he found a switch. He clicked it.

Old furniture. There was nothing in the shed but

piles of old furniture. Looked like stuff that dated from the twenties or thirties, dark and solid.

There was nothing in the shed to cause the revulsion of feeling he felt. Why would Nolie, whose whole farm was a testament to the joy she took in her work, have a rundown shed filled with stuff that should have been gotten rid of years ago?

Then Claire's words clicked in his mind. He'd said Nolie was over the past. She'd disagreed, and here was the evidence.

This wasn't just castoff furniture. These were her great-aunt's things. Nolie said she was over the past, but she'd never gotten rid of them.

Not only that. Judging by the state of the path, she came in here. Relived the past she claimed to have forgotten.

An old-fashioned leather photo album lay on the oak dresser next to the door. He flipped it open, turning the crumbling pages.

The old man in his dark suit and high collar must be the great-great-uncle who'd tied up the property. Judging by the look of him, he'd been typical of the thrifty German farmers who'd turned this part of Pennsylvania into a thriving farming area.

He flipped a few more pages, then stopped, hand frozen on the page. This was a different era on the farm, judging by the car that stood in the lane.

The sour-faced woman who had to be Nolie's great-aunt stood a couple of paces behind a wild-eyed, bearded character who looked like someone's screwy idea of an Old Testament prophet. This was Brother Joshua, presumably. He had the air of a fanatic who'd sacrifice anyone and anything to his version of the truth.

Another figure stood beside the aunt, head bent in a subservient posture. The child's slight frame was shrouded in an ugly dark dress that fell to her ankles, and her hair had been completely covered by a black scarf. Nolie.

A wave of nausea swept over him. He'd listened. He'd sympathized. And he hadn't had the faintest idea of what she'd gone through.

Max leaned against him, whining a little, and then looked through the open door toward the sunshine.

"I know what you mean, Max. There's something pretty sick in here." It was as if a miasma of misery and evil clung to the very furniture.

Poor Nolie. She'd said she was over her past, but Claire was right. She clearly wasn't over it, not when she kept her past locked up in this shed.

And Claire was right about something else. Nolie was vulnerable. He had to be careful.

That thought was still uppermost in Gabe's mind an hour later, when he closed the cottage door behind him and Max. He straightened his tie.

"What do you think, Max? Will we do?"

Max waved his tail. The dog probably felt more at home in the company they were going to encounter tonight than he did. Well, like it or not, he'd promised. He stepped off the porch, Max at his heels.

They crossed the lawn toward the farmhouse. Its lighted windows sent a welcoming glow across the grass. He couldn't help a glance toward the shed. The barn's bulk hid it, but he knew it was there now. He couldn't forget about it any more than Nolie could.

How did anyone get over a childhood experience like hers? He felt momentarily ashamed of his happy childhood. He'd had it so easy, compared to what Nolie had gone through. Alone. She'd done it alone and come out a whole person, but she had her scars. She had to, even though she functioned well.

Just be careful, he warned himself. Now that he understood, it was more important than ever that he resist that attraction that tugged at him each time he was near her. There were too many barriers between them in any event, and this put the final piece of the barricade in place.

Arranging an impersonal smile on his face, he rapped on the door.

"Come in." Nolie's voice echoed faintly.

He opened the front door and stepped into the living room, Max beside him. He closed the door, glancing around. He'd been in the farmhouse kitchen a number of times, but he hadn't been in this room.

Obviously Nolie's redecorating efforts had been at work here. The multi-paned windows were draped with crisp white ruffled curtains, and a colorful rag rug brightened the wide planks of the floor. Everything about the room, from the buttery-soft leather sofa to the built-in bookshelves crowded with books to the wide brick hearth said that this space was designed for the comfort and happiness of the person who lived here.

What had it been like during Nolie's childhood? Nothing like this, that was certain. She'd wiped her aunt's baleful presence from the room, maybe even from the farmhouse, but she hadn't been able to get rid of it entirely. It lingered in that rundown shed.

Would he ever tell her that he'd seen it? Probably not. To do so would be admitting to a depth of relationship that wasn't possible for them. That was why Claire had sent him there. She'd wanted him to see that he wasn't the man for Nolie.

"Sorry if I kept you waiting." Nolie came quickly down the stairs, hand running along the polished rail.

He took a strangled breath, feeling as if someone had just punched him in the stomach. Maybe Claire should have thought twice about what Nolie was wearing tonight if she wanted him to stay away from her. That clingy black dress accentuated every delectable curve of Nolie's body, and the skirt flirted around legs that certainly looked different in black stockings than they did in jeans.

She'd reached the bottom, and she was looking at him strangely. He had to say something.

"I wasn't here long." Surprisingly, his voice sounded almost normal. "Max and I didn't have to do all that much to get ready."

"Well, you both look very nice." Her gaze swept over his dark suit. Approving, he thought. He straightened his tie again.

"I only put a suit on for weddings and funerals. Good thing it still fits."

"I wish I hadn't had to do much to get ready. Claire can go from office to party in ten minutes flat, but she's in practice. This took a lot of work."

"It was worth it." He may as well tell her the truth. "You look breathtaking."

Color flooded her cheeks. "Thank you."

"You're welcome." His tie seemed to be strangling him. "Well, are we ready to go knock them dead at this thing?"

"Not quite." She held out her hand, a chain dangling from it. "Claire insisted on this necklace with the dress, but I can't get it fastened. Will you give me a hand?"

"Sure." He tried to sound casual as he fumbled with the cobweb-fine chain.

Nolie turned her back to him, sweeping that silky fall of pale gold hair away from the nape of her neck. All he wanted to do was press his lips against that smooth curve of skin.

Concentrate, he commanded himself. He swung the necklace around her neck, careful not to touch her. If Nolie knew the longing that pounded through his veins, she'd run screaming from the house. That would certainly be safer.

His fingers brushed the nape of her neck as he fumbled with the catch. It was so fine he nearly dropped it, but that wasn't why his fingers didn't seem to work.

He leaned a little closer, inhaling the flowery scent that clung to her skin. A bit nearer, and he'd give in to the temptation to drop a kiss. Except that it would amount to more than that, and he knew it.

He fastened the clasp, letting his fingertips linger for a moment against her warm, smooth skin. The Nolie he'd seen in that photograph hadn't had anything pretty to wear, or anyone to tell her how lovely she was. She hadn't had any evenings of innocent enjoyment.

So he'd take her to the foundation party, and he'd

see to it that she had a good time. He'd do everything she wanted him to do tonight.

But he wouldn't give in to the longing to have her in his arms—he wasn't going to be the one to hurt her.

Chapter Eleven

Nolie glanced at the dashboard clock as she pulled between the lion-headed gate posts at Townsend Manor. "We're a few minutes late."

"Looks like a lot of people are fashionably late." Gabe nodded toward the cars ahead of them that clogged the circular drive.

Her fingers felt damp against the steering wheel. "I don't know much about this place. No one's ever invited me to anything here before."

"There was a piece in the paper about it when the family donated the estate to the city. Supposed to be pretty elegant. The original Townsend made his money in railroads back when that meant you should build the fanciest place you could afford to show how rich you were."

The house came into view as she pulled around the curving drive toward a portico where uniformed attendants waited to take the car.

"Valet parking, no less." That just increased her

bad case of butterflies. "My van is really going to look out of place in the midst of all those luxury sedans."

"Hey." Gabe reached across to clasp her hand in a brief message of support. "When this place was in its heyday, the only Irishman who'd be here would have been a coachman. Times change. You don't have anything to be embarrassed about."

Before she could respond, the attendant was opening her door. She slid out, waiting while Gabe and Max came around the car to join her. He took her arm, his touch sending a shiver sliding along her skin.

"Relax," he said softly. "It's just a house."

She glanced at the cream-and-yellow mansion that loomed over them. A stream of couples moved through the double doors onto a wide expanse of light-splashed marble. The glittering chandelier set up answering sparkles from sequined dresses.

"Trust me, that is *not* just a house. And these are not just people. Not to a country mouse like me."

Gabe drew her hand through the crook of his arm, so that it rested on his sleeve. She felt the reassuring strength of him through the smooth fabric of his dark suit.

"We're here for a reason. Just keep that in mind. At least no one will try to throw Max out tonight."

His muscles tensed as he spoke, and she knew what he was thinking. He was afraid of having a public seizure in front of all these people.

She wasn't much better. She was afraid of Brother Joshua leaping out of the crowd to call her a harlot for wearing makeup and a pretty dress. They made quite a pair.

The line of people moved forward, carrying them

with it. She took a deep breath. Okay. If Gabe could conquer his demons enough to go through with this, so could she. She had too much at stake to give in to her fears tonight.

But she was glad for the support of Gabe's arm, pressing against her as they walked into the wide center hallway.

The Townsend place was just as elegant as it looked from the outside. The Townsend family had apparently donated the furnishings along with the house, and a marble-topped sideboard had been pressed into service to hold white place cards bearing names in graceful calligraphy.

Gabe reached out to pluck a card with their names on it from its place. "Table Ten. With a little luck, that won't be right in the front."

"I suppose there's not a chance we'll actually know anyone at the table." She hoped she didn't sound as out of place as she felt.

Gabe shrugged. "You never can tell. Let's see what it looks like."

Arm in arm, with Max padding sedately at Gabe's heels, they followed the crowd through a wide archway into a ballroom that ran the length of the building.

"Wow." She couldn't find another word.

Elegantly dressed couples mingled across the polished wood floor, finding seats at round, white-linen-covered tables. Candle flames echoed the glittering points of light from crystal chandeliers. Rows of white columns marched down either side of the room, setting off dimly lit alcoves.

Gabe stared at the marble statue of a female form in Greek robes that peered out from the nearest alcove, and then the corner of his mouth lifted. "Looks as if they borrowed this lot from the Parthenon. Or a Hollywood set."

The humor in his voice lightened her mood. "Funny to think of someone actually living like this, isn't it?"

He grinned at her. "You mean you wouldn't trade the chickens and the donkey for a few columns?"

"Not a chance. But I can enjoy it for one night."

He patted her hand. "That's right. Just remember, we're in this together."

He didn't mean anything by that. Of course he didn't. They weren't really the partners his words had implied. Still, she couldn't stem the warmth they engendered.

They crossed the room, glancing at table numbers until they found the right table. One glance at the six people already seated sent her nerves chattering again, but Gabe seemed perfectly at ease. Apparently he knew one of the men from some civic organization, which eased the introductions to the rest of them.

Nolie smiled, nodded and slipped into her seat with a silent prayer of thanksgiving for Gabe's presence. She'd have gotten through this evening alone, if she'd had to, but Gabe certainly made it easier. Maybe she'd be better off not to dwell on why that was.

Superficial conversation flowed around the table. She knew perfectly well that the other people were curious about the dog, but no one was impolite enough to ask. It was almost a relief when the clink of a spoon on glass drew everyone's attention to the head table.

Her tension peaked. She'd been warned that she would be introduced at this point. Thank heavens no one expected her to say anything—just stand and smile. She could do that.

Samuel Henley beamed around the room as he welcomed everyone as warmly as if they were guests in his private home. He spoke briefly about the work of the foundation and then glanced down at a card on the podium.

"Now I'd like to introduce one of the candidates for this year's grant. Please welcome Nolie Lang, director of Nolie's Ark, a program training service animals to assist people with disabilities."

It's sinful to call attention to yourself. Sinful.

Somehow she couldn't totally eliminate the tape of her aunt's voice that played in the back of her mind. But the quick, hard squeeze of Gabe's fingers on hers seemed to give her energy as she stood.

She managed a smile as people clapped. They applauded for the program, not for her, but she actually seemed to catch a gleam of admiration in the eyes that were on her.

She sank back into her chair with relief, her gaze meeting Gabe's. Her breath caught. It was really unfortunate that the only look of admiration that meant anything to her was the one shining in Gabe's eyes.

Much to Gabe's surprise, the evening had actually gone pretty well. Once the meal and the speeches were over, people circulated, chatting. Clearly they assumed, given Nolie's introduction, that Max was a service dog, but no one asked for what.

Maybe they weren't even thinking that Max was *his* service dog. It was possible they thought the dog had been brought for display, and that her human companion was here as Nolie's date.

He looked at her. She'd begun to relax, apparently realizing that no one was going to chase her out of here. Her eyes sparkled as she explained something about her program to a questioner, but she glanced over the man's shoulder to meet his eyes, giving him a small, private smile.

His heart jolted. She was just too beautiful for his peace of mind, and the fact that her beauty extended all the way to her soul didn't help any. He had to remind himself that his purpose tonight was to help Nolie without getting too close.

A jazz quartet was playing in the corner, and couples had begun to move onto the dance floor. Nolie made her way to his side. She nodded toward the dancers.

"What do you say? Claire dragged me to ballroom dance classes a couple of years ago, but I've never had a chance to practice what I learned."

Holding Nolie in his arms was certainly not the best way to keep his distance. But she was looking at him with stars shining in her eyes, and he didn't want to disappoint her.

"What will Max do while we dance?" He tried for a light touch. "You know you're his best girl. He might be jealous."

Max looked up at the sound of his name and gave them a wide doggy grin.

"He'll have to get along without me when he goes home with his partner, anyway." She was obviously being careful not to make assumptions about Max going home with him. "I'll probably be the one who does most of the missing."

Her words touched his heart. "It's hard to say goodbye to animals you've come to love."

"It's part of the job." Her eyes were shadowed for a moment. Maybe she was thinking that she had to say goodbye to people she'd learned to love, as well. "Just tell him to stay."

"Stay, Max."

He shouldn't hold Nolie in his arms. He was going to. He held out his hand to her and led her onto the dance floor.

They moved smoothly, as if they'd danced together many times before and would again. She was warm and sweet in his arms, and when she looked at him his breath caught at her beauty.

They circled the room slowly to the music, feet whispering on the polished floor. The other couples faded to a moving background against which he and Nolie danced, lost in each other's eyes. He could feel the movement of her breathing through the hand he pressed against her back, and even their breathing was in tandem.

They moved between two of the pillars, out of the stream of dancers for the moment. His steps slowed, and he lifted his hand to touch the strand of pale gold hair that lay against her shoulder.

"Beautiful. You know that, don't you?"

Instead of a smile, something dark and pained crossed her face. She shook her head in a short, choppy movement.

He drew her a little closer. "Nolie? What is it? What did I say?"

"Nothing."

But it was something. He could see that. "You can tell me. Please."

She glanced toward the dancers. "Not here."

French doors stood open behind them, letting a warm spring breeze into the room. Clasping her hand, he pulled her through the opening onto a dimly lit veranda.

"Now tell me." He wasn't sure what pushed him. He only knew he had to erase that pain from her eyes if he could.

She put a hand up to her hair. "I shouldn't let it bother me after all this time. I don't even know why I thought of it."

The words were dismissive, but the pain wasn't. It throbbed like a wound under her voice, and he knew he was right to push the issue.

"Because it still hurts. Tell me what they did to you."

She turned away as if she didn't want to look at him, her profile delicately beautiful in the moonlight and fragile as glass.

"I was about thirteen. I guess Brother Joshua noticed I wasn't a little girl anymore. He grabbed me one day out behind the barn." A shudder went through her. "He kissed me. I don't know what else he might have done, but my aunt came out and caught us."

"Caught him," he corrected, managing to keep his voice gentle in spite of the anger that raced through his veins like fire. "You didn't do anything wrong."

"That's not how they saw it." Her throat worked with the effort to swallow. "He said it was my fault. Said my hair was an invitation to vanity and a trap for men." Her fingers seemed to have tangled in the lock of hair. "So they chopped it off in a crewcut, like a boy's."

His fury at them was like a backdraft, sending a wall of flame soaring, destroying everything in its path. It was probably good they were both dead, or he'd have wanted to track them down and punish them himself.

Somehow he choked the anger down. He clasped her fingers, drawing them gently free of her hair and then stroking the lock of hair smooth again.

"They were wrong," he said when he could trust himself to speak. "Criminally wrong. Evil. You do know that, don't you?"

She nodded. "I know that intellectually. Sometimes my emotions are a different story, though. I hear their voices when I least expect it."

He touched her cheek gently, turning her face toward him. "That's letting them win. You can't let them win."

"I try. Believe me, I try." She looked up at him then, her eyes huge and lost.

He was lost, too. He couldn't stop caring for her, no matter how impossible it was.

And he couldn't stop the urge to kiss her. It wasn't the wise thing to do, but he couldn't help himself.

His palm cradled her cheek, and her skin was silk against his. "Nolie." He said her name softly, watching her eyes darken as she realized he was going to kiss her.

Her lips parted, and the pulse in her neck hammered against his hand. Neither of them could stop this. It was inevitable.

His lips found hers, and she moved into his arms with a tiny sigh. His hands moved on the silky stuff of her dress, then on the warm, smooth skin of her shoulders. He drew her even closer, shaken by the storm of emotions that demanded he hold her, protect her, keep her close by his side forever.

Forever. The word was like a spray of cold water. Nolie, sweet, vulnerable Nolie, would expect forever. He couldn't hurt her.

He touched her face again, drawing back a fraction of an inch, and pressed a line of kisses across her cheek. His brain and his body didn't seem able to work together. He had to stop. But maybe he'd at least managed to wipe out that ugly memory and replace it with a better one.

"Nolie." He said her name more firmly as he forced his lips away from her skin. "You are a beautiful, desirable woman. They don't have power over you anymore." He stroked her hair. "They're gone, and you're here. You're a success. You won."

Her eyes were huge and more than a little dazed. She drew back slightly, still in the circle of his arms. He saw reason replace the dazed look, and he knew it was time to move onto firmer ground.

He had to. But it was tempting, so tempting, to stay right here in the clouds with Nolie in his arms.

She couldn't let Gabe know how much his kisses had affected her. Nolie took a careful step backward, cold suddenly at the distance between them.

She didn't want the moment to end, but it had to. She could see that in Gabe's eyes. He was already wondering why he'd kissed her, probably reminding himself of the distance between them and the disagreement that seemed so irrevocable.

Even if things could work out between them, now wasn't the time. Maybe, after Gabe's training was finished, but not now. And probably once he was free of the training program, he wouldn't want her in his life as a constant reminder of this difficult time.

"Maybe we ought to go back inside." She managed to keep her voice as calm as if she hadn't just been rocked to her very soul by his kisses. "We are working tonight, after all."

"Right." Gabe moved away a step, as careful as she had been. "Max is probably wondering where we are."

That's right. Take this lightly. Pretend you haven't just been kissing the man you can't help loving.

She turned and let him pilot her back into the room. The dancers still circled, the lights still shone. They might never have been gone.

But they had. And she, at least, had been changed by what had happened between them. She could only hope she didn't wear a starry-eyed look that would alert everyone in the room to what they'd been doing.

Max, ears pricked forward, watched them as they approached. His velvet eyes seemed to look at them knowingly.

Well, even if Max knew, he couldn't tell anyone.

Besides, there was nothing wrong with kissing Gabe. Even if nothing ever came of it, it wasn't wrong to kiss him.

As Claire had said, they wouldn't be working together forever. Then—well, then she'd see. If Gabe wanted to continue seeing her, he knew where she was.

"Good boy, Maxie." She patted her knee, letting the dog know it was okay to get up.

He stood, stretching elaborately, then walked over to Gabe and sat down at his side, waiting for Gabe's praise. Gabe ruffled his ears.

"Good boy."

She tried to ignore the slight pang in her heart. Max was transferring his allegiance to Gabe. That was the way it should be. Now, if she could just make Gabe see that the dog should continue to be a part of his life, she probably shouldn't ask for more.

Gabe lifted an eyebrow as he looked toward her, his hand on Max's head. "What do you think? Can we blow this joint yet?"

People were starting to filter out the doors. "I guess so. As far as I know, my duties ended with being introduced. Everything else was icing."

The meal, the dancing, that was what she meant. She certainly didn't mean being kissed senseless on the veranda, did she?

Gabe handed her the small black evening bag Claire had provided with the dress. "I guess we're ready, then."

They'd reached the hallway when Nolie saw a rotund figure in a black tuxedo hurrying toward them.

"Ms. Lang. Mr. Flanagan." Mr. Henley extended a hand to each of them. "I'm glad you were able to make it tonight." He was as gracious as if this hadn't been a command performance. "I hope you enjoyed yourselves."

"It was a lovely event." She could only hope her

heightened color didn't give away which part of the evening she'd found most lovely. ''Thank you for inviting us.''

''A pleasure.'' His attention had shifted to Max. ''And this is one of your talented animals.''

''This is Max, the dog who has been training with Mr. Flanagan.''

He held out his hand to Max, who sniffed politely and then let himself be patted. ''He's quite the gentleman, isn't he?'' He glanced at Gabe, making it clear that he expected a response from him. ''Or shouldn't I be patting him when he's on duty?''

''It's all right.''

Gabe's answer wasn't exactly forthcoming, but at least he'd said something.

''We don't encourage people to play with a seizure-alert dog when he's on duty, but it won't distract him to be introduced.'' She hoped her explanation masked Gabe's shortness.

Mr. Henley nodded gravely. ''I see.'' Again he looked at Gabe. ''And how is the training working out?''

Please. She found herself pleading silently with Gabe. Say something positive. Please.

''It's going very well.'' Gabe seemed to respond to her thoughts. ''Max is a well-trained animal, and the work Nolie does with her clients and the animals is really amazing.'' He patted Max. ''I hope you're going to look favorably on her grant request. Having seen her work in action, I can only say she deserves it.''

She'd be more gratified by his words if he weren't

putting himself so carefully out of the picture. Still, she should be happy he was willing to say that much.

"We're looking forward to seeing that in person." Henley smiled, carefully evasive.

"Seeing it in person?" she echoed. What was he talking about?

"Well, naturally the board won't be willing to give so substantial a grant without a demonstration of your program in action," Henley said.

Naturally.

She swallowed. "I thought you were just expecting a report on Mr. Flanagan's experience with the program."

He swept that aside with an expansive gesture. "Reports are all very well, but nothing substitutes for seeing the program ourselves. I'll have my secretary call you to set up a time for the board to visit."

"Of course. Anytime." What else could she say? She didn't have to look at Gabe to guess his response to the idea.

"We'll have a look around your facility, and you can show us exactly what you do. Of course, seeing Mr. Flanagan work with the dog and hearing his testimony will be the highlight of the visit."

"I'm not sure—"

He clapped Gabe on the shoulder, seeming not to notice how stiff he was. "There's nothing like hearing from a disabled hero to sway public opinion, as I'm sure you realize."

Luckily Gabe didn't say anything, since whatever he might say to the idea was probably unprintable.

"Thank you. I'll look forward to seeing you, then." She edged past the man, grateful when his attention seemed to be caught by someone behind them. Gabe was already halfway out the door, and she scurried after him.

She didn't catch up with him until she reached the bottom of the steps, where he was handing the ticket to the parking attendant. The man trotted off, leaving them momentarily alone in the dim light.

Still, it didn't take too much light to decipher the expression on Gabe's face. He was furious.

"I didn't know that was what the foundation board had in mind." She hurried to get the words out first. "No one ever said they expected a demonstration."

"It doesn't matter." He clipped the words off.

She could only stare at him. "It doesn't?"

"It doesn't matter whether you expected it or not. I won't do it."

Her heart sank. She'd known that would be his reaction, but—

"Gabe, you heard him. He's looking forward to seeing you work with Max. That's not too much to ask, is it?"

He looked at her as if she'd suggested he leap off the barn roof. "He doesn't want a simple display of what the dog can do. If he did, you could give a better demonstration with Danny and Lady, you know that."

"But—"

"He wants testimony. You heard him. He wants testimony from the disabled hero." He spat the words out. "He wants me to get up there and talk about how I have to depend on the dog to get me through the day."

You do, Gabe. Why won't you realize that?

''I won't do it. If I stood up in public and said that, it would mean an end to my career. I can't. And I won't.''

His voice was flat. Final.

Chapter Twelve

Her Cinderella moment was over. Nolie drove down the narrow blacktop leading to the farm, trying her best to hold her pain at bay. She would not let herself dwell on the contrast between how she'd felt leaving for the foundation affair and how she felt now. Her joy in the pretty dress had vanished as thoroughly as the admiration in Gabe's eyes.

She could do nothing about that. Perhaps she could still do something about Gabe's attitude.

The stark reality was that if he backed out of the program now, she could lose the grant. But if he did what Henley asked, he felt he'd lose his future. They couldn't both get what they wanted.

The difference between them lay in Gabe's inability to admit the truth about his situation. Probably she couldn't change that, but she had to try one last time.

She drew up by the house and glanced at Gabe as she turned off the ignition. His face was brooding and withdrawn.

"Can we talk for a few minutes before you go to the cottage?"

He reached for the door handle. "It won't do any good."

He was closed to her, perhaps completely, perhaps forever. But she couldn't give up.

"Please." She put her hand on his arm. "Just for a few minutes."

Max whined softly, either because he didn't understand why they hadn't gotten out of the car or because he sensed the tension between them.

Gabe jerked a short nod, then got out quickly, letting the dog out.

She came around the car slowly, trying to arrange her thoughts in some coherent manner. The night air was cool on her arms. She nodded toward the porch swing, sheltered from the breeze.

"Let's sit down."

Max, released from confinement in the car, began to nose around the bushes. Gabe looked as if he longed for similar release, but he followed her to the porch. She sat on the cushioned swing, feeling it rock as Gabe took his place next to her.

The cool air brought the faint scent of roses to her. Sitting here with Gabe could have been a lovely, romantic moment. It was anything but that.

"I know what you're going to say, Nolie. I want you to get the grant. But I can't do what Henley wants."

She tried to think what arguments might persuade him, but her mind seemed blank. "Maybe the results wouldn't be as bad as you think. Surely the chief understands the position he's put you in."

Gabe put his elbows on his knees, clasping his hands. In the dim light he was a solid, dark bulk, immovable as a rock.

"They're talking about publicity, you must know that. Publicity for the foundation."

"They survive on contributions. Publicity brings in the money that keeps good programs afloat."

His face turned toward hers. "They do good work. They deserve good press. But not at the cost of my life."

"It wouldn't necessarily—"

"If I let them use me as some kind of poster boy, I'll never get back on active duty." His voice was heavy. Final.

She had to say the truth, even though she knew it would hurt him. "You may not have a choice. You can't be a firefighter if you're suffering from seizures."

He jerked as if she'd shot him. "I won't. I'll take the medicine if I have to, but I'm going back on the job. It's my life."

He really believed that. She thought she understood why, but—

"I understand the chief is willing to give you a desk job in the department."

"No." His anger came toward her in a black wave. "I'm a firefighter, not a desk jockey."

Her throat ached with the need to reach him. "I know helping people is your life. Maybe God has a way for you to do that that you haven't considered."

"You sound like Brendan. I should listen to what God wants for me. But you know what? Ever since the accident, I've been trying to reach Him. And He's been silent.''

She heard the pain that threaded his voice—heard it and didn't know how to respond. She had to force herself to reach back, far back into the painful past she didn't want to remember.

She took a breath, steadied herself. She'd told Gabe so much. She could tell him this much more.

''I felt that way once—that God had abandoned me. That He didn't hear my pain.'' She had to force the words out one at a time, they hurt so much. ''It wasn't until I was desperate enough to express my anger at God that I found I'd taken that first step toward healing. God was big enough to take my anger and love me anyway.''

His head came up in a swift, instinctive response. ''Don't tell me what to do, Nolie. You're not all that healed when you can't even get rid of your aunt's belongings.''

His words hit her like a blow. He knew. Gabe knew about the contents of the shed. Knew, and thought her a coward or a weakling for not doing something about it.

She was still grappling with the pain when he surged off the swing, setting it rocking violently. He stood in front of her, hands shoved into his pockets, head lowered.

''I'm sorry. I shouldn't have said that.''

She dismissed the apology with a flicker of her fingers. ''It doesn't matter.'' She took a breath, trying to get a handle on her pain. ''What matters is the work. That's all that matters.''

No, that wasn't all that mattered. It also mattered

that she loved him. But loving him wasn't going to change anything between them.

"You're doing good work. I know that. But I won't sacrifice my future for it. I can't."

He turned. Stepped off the porch. He was going, and she couldn't stop him.

She took a breath, pushed herself upright. Max, with a last look at her, trotted after Gabe.

She could call the dog back, but she wouldn't. He was the one frail thread that still connected Gabe to her work.

Unfortunately, she couldn't make herself believe that was going to make a difference. There was nothing left for her and Gabe.

Gabe stood at the cottage window Monday morning, looking out at the farm. A last look? He'd thought that yesterday. After church with the family he'd seriously considered packing his things and moving back home.

But he'd committed himself to sticking with the program for another week. If he dropped out before then the chief would be furious. Any chance that he'd look favorably on Gabe's return to active duty would disappear.

He rubbed the back of his neck, where tension had taken up permanent residence since he'd learned what the foundation expected of him. There had to be a solution that would let him and Nolie get what they wanted.

The only possibility he saw was a slim one. He could finish the training, then appear at the little dog-and-pony show for the foundation and tell them that while he was well now and didn't need a service dog, he had nothing but praise for Nolie's program.

Unfortunately Nolie could blow that out of the water by telling them about his last seizure. Would she?

Analyzing Nolie's reactions was a risky thing. If she agreed to cooperate with him—well, at least then she'd stand a chance of getting her funding. Otherwise—

He found he didn't want to think of that. They'd both been put in an unfair position. He didn't want to be the one to blow her chances at the grant. She did good work.

He put his hand against the glass, frowning. He'd seen Nolie and Danny go into the barn a few minutes ago. The kid was crazy about the animals, and that was often his reward for a good session.

A car was coming up the lane, fast. It should be Danny's mother coming back for him, but that wasn't her van.

The car shrieked to a stop, spraying gravel. A man surged out, slamming the car door. Danny's father.

Tension shot along his nerves. From what he'd gathered, the father was opposed to Danny's work with the dog. He'd never come to pick him up before. What was he doing here now?

The man charged toward the training center, but then stopped, his body swinging toward the barn. He must have heard their voices. He veered that way, his head down like a charging bull.

Trouble.

The word was like the alarm, calling him to action. He yanked the door open, hearing the rush of Max's feet as he scrabbled across the floor to join him. Not bothering to shut the door, he leaped over the stepping stones of the path and raced across the lawn toward the barn.

The man was out of sight already. He should have moved faster, should have recognized that the father's arrival wasn't normal. Nolie and Danny were alone in the barn, facing a man whose anger had been evident in every line of his body.

Max reached the doorway before he did and stopped, letting out a volley of barking fiercer than any Gabe had heard before. The dog lunged forward.

"Max, stay!" He thundered the command. Whatever was happening, he could handle it with more reason than Max could.

Then he reached the doorway. The father was reaching for Danny, but Nolie stood in his way, her slim frame dwarfed by his bulk. Before Gabe could get another word out, the man had thrust her aside with a single sweep of his arm. Nolie stumbled, lost her footing, and hit the barn floor hard.

The sight was like the fierce blast of air from a fire, propelling him toward them so fast he didn't think his feet touched the ground. He grabbed the man, adrenaline pumping, muscles bunching, fury eclipsing every other emotion. His fist clenched.

"Gabe, no."

Nolie's voice was probably the only thing in the world that could have stopped him. He spun the man around, grasping him by both arms, and looked toward Nolie.

She scrambled to her feet, her face white. "I'm all right." She was probably trying to sound normal for Danny's sake, but it wasn't working.

"Are you sure?" His voice was rough with emotion. If she'd been hurt—

"I'm fine." Her gaze telegraphed a warning. *Not in front of Danny.* "I just stumbled, that's all."

Judging by the kid's expression, he knew perfectly well that wasn't all.

"You okay, Danny?"

The boy managed a nod.

"That's good."

He glanced toward Nolie for direction. His grand heroic gesture seemed to be dwindling to farce. Now he had the guy, but what was he going to do with him? The fury still pumped along his veins, but manhandling the man in front of his kid wasn't a possibility.

"Maybe you ought to take Danny's father to his car. Danny won't be going with him today." Nolie had reached the wheelchair, and she put one arm protectively around the boy's shoulders.

He nodded, turning the man toward the door. Max, hackles raised and a low growl rumbling in his throat, followed them as he propelled Danny's father out of the barn.

I know what you feel, boy. I do, too. But Nolie wouldn't thank us for making any more of a scene, so I guess we just have to play it her way.

Nolie took a deep breath, searching for strength. She had to be calm for Danny's sake, no matter what she'd felt.

But those terrifying moments when Danny's father had stormed into the barn weren't easy to erase. It hadn't taken a moment to know that the man had been drinking and was totally irrational. He'd been determined to take Danny. All she'd known was that she couldn't let him, no matter what.

She'd have failed. If Gabe hadn't come through that doorway like an avenging angel, she wouldn't have been able to prevent it.

She'd never seen anything to match the fury in Gabe's eyes. For a moment she'd been afraid of what he might do.

But that had been foolish. No matter how he was provoked, Gabe would never lose control of himself enough to hurt anyone.

Thank you, Father.

She hugged Danny, feeling the tension in his thin shoulders. "Are you okay, Danny? I know that was upsetting, but everything's all right now."

"Gabe won't hurt my daddy, will he?"

"No, of course not. He'll just give your dad time to cool off, that's all." She hesitated, not sure how much more to say. "Your mom should be here in a few minutes, and she'll take you home. I'll bet your dad will be feeling a lot better by the next time you see him."

Danny nodded, but she read the pain in his eyes.

Poor child. His love for his father was battling the feeling that he'd somehow let him down.

"I'm sorry," he mumbled.

Please, Father. Give me the words.

"You know, Danny, sometimes we feel responsible when someone we love does something hurtful." She stroked his hair. "But it's not your fault when that happens."

What had happened to her hadn't been her fault, but she'd still carried the burden of it for a long time.

She cupped his chin in her hand, looking into his eyes. "It's never your fault when grown-ups don't act the way they should. You remember that, okay?"

He nodded solemnly.

She hugged him, hoping she'd done enough to ease his pain. Wishing she could take it away entirely. Danny bore his burdens with courage. If only his father could do the same.

Her throat tightened. How was Gabe handling the stress of the incident? It couldn't be good for him. If it triggered a seizure—

She heard voices, two of them, and her tension eased. It was Gabe, and it sounded as if Danny's mother was with him.

"Hey, Danny." Gabe came straight to the boy. "You okay, buddy?"

He nodded. "Is my daddy okay?"

"He's fine. He's just embarrassed about the way he acted, you know? He's kind of upset, so I called a taxi to take him home."

Myra touched her son's shoulder, and her expression mingled hurt and apology. "It'll be all right, Danny. I promise."

"Nolie says it's not my fault if grown-ups don't act the way they should." He watched his mother, as if waiting for her reaction to that.

She managed a smile that trembled on the verge of tears. "Nolie's exactly right. Come on, now. Let's go home." She glanced at Nolie. "I'm sorry," she said softly. "If I'd been on time, it wouldn't have happened. Traffic was held up out by Forest Road. It looked like there's a fire.''

Nolie felt the sharp surge of Gabe's attention as surely as if they were touching.

''Did you see where it was?'' He rapped out the question.

Myra shook her head, pushing Danny toward the door. ''We'll just go around by Fifteenth Street on our way home.''

Nolie waited until they were out of earshot. ''Would your brothers have gone on the call?''

''Not unless it went to several alarms. That's not their district. Times like this, I miss the radio. Even if it's not my fire, I always want to hear about it.'' He shrugged. ''Still, I guess there was enough excitement here for one day.''

''Definitely.'' He wouldn't want to be thanked, but she had to say it. ''Thank you. I don't know how I'd have handled Danny's father if you hadn't been here.'' She hesitated, but she might as well say the rest of it. ''I thought you might have left.''

''You thought I'd have bailed out.'' He shook his head. ''I haven't changed my mind about performing for the foundation. But I said I'd see the training through, and I will.''

Probably only because of the pressure from his chief, but she had to be grateful for anything that kept him here a bit longer.

''What happened with Danny's father when you took him outside?''

Gabe leaned back against the stall door, propping one heel against the rail. ''Not much.''

She raised her eyebrows. ''I heard what you told

Danny. Now tell me the things you didn't want to say to him.''

His face eased. ''Well, I certainly didn't want to tell the kid that I felt like punching his old man.''

''You didn't—''

''No, I didn't. But when I saw him shove you to the floor, I certainly wanted to. Are you sure you're all right?''

She nodded, rubbing her shoulder. ''I landed a little hard, but I'm okay.''

''Let me.'' He reached out to massage her shoulder, his hand warm and gentle. ''You shouldn't take on guys who are twice your size.''

''I'll remember that the next time.'' And she'd remember forever the way she felt at Gabe's touch.

''Don't let there be a next time.'' He was frowning again. ''It's not your job to deal with the parents' problems.''

''Unfortunately Danny's father thinks I'm part of the problem. He doesn't want Danny involved in the program.''

''I know. He told me that.''

''He talked to you about it?'' She'd never heard Danny's father willingly discuss his son's condition.

Gabe stroked her shoulder. ''He started to. Then all of a sudden he broke down in tears.'' Gabe's voice thickened, as if his own tears weren't far away. ''Poor jerk. He's trying to protect his kid, but he doesn't know how to do it.''

''What did you say to him?''

''I thought about my dad. Funny. I mean, we've never been in a situation like that, but I still thought about what he'd do, if one of his kids had been disabled."

Joe and Siobhan Flanagan were devoted to their kids. She hadn't had to be around them long to see that. "What did you come up with?"

"I told him the best way he could help his son was to set an example of strength, not one of weakness. And that he wasn't going to find strength in a bottle."

She could only nod. Gabe had given the man good advice, if he could find a way to follow it.

"You set a pretty good example of strength yourself, you know."

He dismissed it with a slight smile. "Didn't take all that much muscle to hustle a drunk out of here."

"That's not the kind of strength I was talking about." If only Gabe could see that his strength could be used for so many things other than fire fighting. "It was stressful, but you handled it."

He shrugged. "I didn't have a seizure. And I wouldn't if I were back on the job, because I thrive on that kind of stress. You have to, if you're a firefighter."

She still thought he was kidding himself, but there was no point in saying it again. "I'm glad you're going to stay out the week. Thank you for that."

"I don't want you to lose the grant, Nolie." His hand on her shoulder tightened. "I'll do anything I can to convince Mr. Henley that you deserve it."

"Anything but tell him you need the dog." They'd come full circle, and nothing had changed.

"I can't do that." He drew her a little closer, and the intensity of his gaze seemed to heat her skin. "You have to understand why I can't."

"I know."

Tears stung her eyes, and her heart overflowed with the love she couldn't speak. She'd do anything if she could only wrap up his heart's desire and give it to him as a present, but she couldn't, any more than she could give Danny limbs that worked.

Either Gabe moved, or she moved, but they were very close. She felt his breath against her cheek.

"I wish—" His voice was a murmur that seemed to fade on the words.

What did he wish? His nearness was robbing her of coherent thought.

His fingers brushed her cheek. In a moment they'd be kissing again.

A sudden shrilling made her eyes fly to his. "What—"

He was already pulling the cell phone from his pocket, brows furrowed.

She managed a strangled breath. It was probably a very good thing his phone had rung just then. Otherwise they'd have found themselves kissing again, and that wasn't going to lead anywhere.

"Where are they?"

The sudden sharpening of Gabe's voice alerted her. Something was wrong.

"I'll be there in ten minutes." He clicked the phone off, already turning toward the door.

"What is it? What's happened?"

The face he turned to her was a rigid mask. "The fire. A three-alarm down at the old shirt factory. Engine 10 was called. The roof collapsed."

Fear grabbed her heart. "Your family?"

"My dad and Ryan. They've both been taken to

Providence Hospital. I don't know how badly they're hurt." He shook his head, his expression breaking into anguish. "I've got to get to them, and I can't even drive."

She was already jerking the ring of keys from her pocket. "I'll take you."

Their feet thudded on the barn floor as they ran, Max leaping along beside them as if it was a game.

No game. Joe. Ryan. Their faces formed in her mind as she ran.

Please, Lord. Please. Hold them in Your hands.

There wasn't anything else to say.

Chapter Thirteen

He'd been praying all the way to the hospital, frantic, almost wordless prayers. He glanced across the front seat. Nolie was praying, too, her lips moving soundlessly.

He snapped off the phone. "Busy. Everyone who's not at the fire is calling everyone else, trying to find out what's happening." He rubbed his forehead. "I don't know who else to try."

He should have been there. *Dad. Ryan.* He tried to swallow the fear that was acid in his throat. He kept forming pictures in his mind. That was the trouble with knowing too much about what could happen.

"That place was a firetrap that should have been torn down years ago." He didn't know whether he was talking to Nolie or to himself. "No sprinklers and a roof that was bound to go once the fire reached it."

"I thought I'd read in the paper that they'd been renovating the building." Nolie seemed to understand that he had to talk or go crazy.

"That probably made it worse. Lots of flammable materials around, and no way of knowing what the contractors had been doing."

Nolie went through an intersection on a yellow light. "Just two blocks." She glanced at him, hesitation in her face. "Do you want me to leave after I drop you off?"

"No." The negative was out before he thought about it. He needed her with him. He didn't want to analyze why.

"Okay." Her response was brief. Maybe she didn't want to think about it, either.

"Mom's going to be devastated. When I got hurt, she had Dad to protect her from the worst of it."

"Your mother's a strong woman. She'll bear anything she has to."

Nolie didn't know his family. She didn't understand that Dad was the strong one. Mom had to be shielded, but in this case he didn't know how that could be managed.

They drew up in front of the hospital, and his stomach turned over. In a few minutes he'd know.

"Just let me out—" he began, but Nolie was already pulling into one of the reserved slots.

"I have a permit because of the work I do." She snapped off the ignition and slid out of the car. She and Max were right behind him as he ran into the emergency room.

"The firefighters from Engine 10. Where are they?"

The woman behind the desk stared at him blankly. "You can't bring a dog in here."

"Max is my seizure-alert dog. You can't deny us

access.'' He said the words without thinking twice. ''My family must be here. Where are they?''

An EMT pushed through the doors from the treatment area and came toward him. He didn't recognize her, but she seemed to know him.

''We put your family in the lounge.'' She pointed toward a swinging door. ''Right through there.''

He pushed through the door and came to a halt, aware of Nolie close behind him.

Mary Kate had her arms around his mother. Brendan sat on the other side of her, his embrace seeming to hold both women. Seth sagged in a chair, still in his turnout coat, his helmet on the floor beside him and his face black.

''How are they?'' His question went to Seth, who surely knew the most, even as he crossed the room to hug his mother.

''Ryan has a broken right arm, some burns. Nothing too serious. He was trapped, but we pulled him out pretty fast.'' Seth's blue eyes were the only alive thing in his face. ''Dad—we don't know yet.''

He couldn't let himself feel thankful for Ryan until he knew about his father.

''What happened? Was he trapped, too?'' A battalion chief shouldn't have been on the front line, but it was tough to hold Dad back, they all knew that.

''No.'' Seth buried his face in his hands, his voice muffled. ''Ryan was first in, on the nozzle. I guess he thought he could go farther. Dad saw the condition of the roof, yelled at him to get back, but maybe he didn't hear.''

Nolie probably didn't understand, but he could translate that without any trouble. Ryan, revved up and running on adrenaline, had gone too far without pausing to analyze the danger.

"Dad went after him, didn't he?"

Seth looked up. "He tried. But the roof came down. By the time we reached Ryan, Dad had collapsed. Paramedics were already there. They brought them both in."

"We just have to wait." His mother patted his arm. "That's all we can do now. Wait."

He met Brendan's eyes over his mother's head. How long would his mother's poise last, with her son and her husband both injured?

"Where's Terry?"

"Her unit was still on duty." Brendan was quickly reassuring. "She figured she could do more good there than here."

Max lay in the corner, his eyes moving from Nolie to Gabe and back again. Nolie had found a coffeemaker on the counter and was quietly putting the pot on. Her gaze caught his, and he nodded. Trust Nolie to find something practical to do.

Maybe that was why he'd instinctively wanted her here. Nolie would be a rock in time of trouble. She'd found her strength the hard way.

He got up, went to her, and started searching the cabinets for cups. "Thanks," he said softly. "That'll help."

"Well, I don't know that it does, really, but it's something to do with your hands." She kept her voice low as she glanced back at Seth. "Your brother ought to be checked out, too. He looks as if he's in shock."

"I know, but he won't leave Mom now. Give me a coffee with extra sugar and I'll take it to him."

She nodded, pouring the coffee. When she gave it to him, he clasped her hand briefly. "Thanks for staying."

"Of course." Her blue eyes had darkened with concern. "Anything I can do. You know that."

He gave a wry smile. "Make another pot. This room will be filled with firefighters as soon as they've knocked down the blaze."

She nodded, but her gaze was questioning.

"That's how it is. Nobody will go home until they've come to the hospital. Firefighters look after their own."

He heard the door swing open and spun around, heart pumping. If it was news about Dad—

It was Ryan. His arm was in a sling and the side of his face red and raw, but otherwise he looked okay.

Gabe's jaw tightened. Hadn't he warned the kid to take care? Ryan hadn't been able to tell the difference between being aggressive and taking unnecessary risks, and look at the result.

Nolie's hand closed over his arm as if she read his thoughts. "There's nothing you can say that will make him feel any worse than he already does," she murmured.

What did she know about it? If he'd gotten through to Ryan, this wouldn't have happened. He jerked his arm free. He'd say anything he wanted to his brother.

Before he could move, Ryan crossed the room in a stumbling run. He dropped to his knees in front of Mom, his face twisting.

"I'm sorry, Mom. I'm sorry." His voice broke in sobs. "It was my fault. Dad wouldn't be here if I—"

Siobhan put her arms around him. "Don't, Ryan,

don't.'' It was the voice she'd used when he'd come home at five or six, crying because he'd wrecked his bike. ''It's not your fault. It will be all right.''

Sobs wracked Ryan's body, and he clutched her like a lifeline.

Gabe's anger went out like a blown candle flame. How many times had Mom said those reassuring words to her kids? *It will be all right.*

He crossed to them and knelt to put his arm across his brother's shoulders.

''It's going to be okay, Ry. It will. It'll take more than this to get the old man down. He'll probably come out of it with another citation.''

He felt his mother stiffen at his words. ''Do you think a citation is worth a hair on his head?'' Anger flared in her eyes. ''Do you?''

''No, of course not.'' He sat back on his heels. ''I'm sorry. I didn't mean to upset you.''

The fire left her gaze. For an instant her lips trembled, but then they firmed. She patted his cheek. ''I know. He's doing what he loves. You all are. But every time you're on the job, I wait for the call.'' She shuddered. ''Or the knock on the door.''

They wouldn't call if it was a fatality. Every firefighter family knew that. The battalion chief would come to the door with the chaplain.

He didn't know what to say. He'd always somehow assumed that Mom didn't really understand how dangerous it was. And he'd certainly never understood how strong she had to be to keep her fear hidden from them all this time.

Nolie had known. He put his arm around his mother, but his gaze sought out Nolie's. She was watching him, her blue eyes bright with tears. Nolie had understood what he hadn't. The thought grabbed his heart and twisted it.

"You were right." Nolie backed up against the counter next to Gabe. "I know you said everyone would come, but I still didn't expect this."

She'd made three pots of coffee, and clearly it wasn't enough for all the people who'd crowded the small lounge. Firefighters, some of their spouses, people from the Flanagans' church—they had all filtered in over the past half hour until it seemed the room could hold no more. Not even the dragon at the reception desk could keep them out.

"Firefighters are family, just like the people from the church are. I knew they'd come as soon as they'd gotten the fire under control." Gabe's eyes darkened. "Thank God no one else was hurt."

"Yes." *Thank You, Father.*

Gabe was holding the fresh cup of coffee she'd handed him, but he wasn't drinking it. He'd probably had enough caffeine to last him for days. Still, he wouldn't be able to rest until he knew his father was all right.

Please, Lord. Be with Joe.

"How often does this kind of thing happen?" And how did the spouses stand it?

"Not often. Not here. A bigger city like Baltimore or Philly has more fires, more injuries." He set the cup down. "We'd go, no matter how far, if a firefighter died on the job. For the funeral. They're our brothers."

Her throat tightened. He'd said they were family,

and clearly he'd meant it. She glanced at Siobhan, sur-
rounded by so much love, so many people who cared
for her. They were hugging her, praying with her, giving her strength.

Who do you have?

The question seared into her brain, shocking her.
Who did she have? Claire. The animals. Not a very
long list. If she were in trouble, who would come to
pray with her?

The crowded room suddenly seemed stifling. "I'm
going to see if I can get some more coffee."

Gabe nodded, his attention claimed by someone else
who'd come up to speak to him. She slipped quickly
from the jammed room.

She paused outside the door, taking a breath. Even
here, the outer doors were opening to let in more people with worried faces. She turned and hurried down
the hall. Surely there was someplace where she could
be alone for a few minutes.

A pair of swinging doors at the end of the hallway
bore a brass sign. Chapel. Something inside her
cringed away from the title, but she wouldn't be a
coward about it. Quickly, before she could change her
mind, she pushed the door open and stepped inside.

The room was small, with five or six rows of pale
wooden pews arranged in front of a simple altar. The
only decoration was a painting depicting Jesus healing
a lame man. Christ's hand was outstretched, and somehow the artist had managed to convey both love and
empathy in His expression.

She couldn't seem to take her eyes off the painting
as she slid into one of the pews. She'd expected to
feel a wave of revulsion at the place, reminding her

of Brother Joshua's chapel. Instead she felt welcomed. At peace.

Was this what Gabe's family felt in their church? She struggled with a wave of longing to have what they did—love, support, family. Even with the accompanying pain, it would be worth it to know you had that.

Tears stung her eyes. She folded her hands on the pew in front of her and pressed her face against her knuckles.

Please, Father, be with Joe and his family now. Strengthen him, and give his doctors wisdom. And help me to understand where You're leading me. I thought I knew how my life was meant to be, but now—

"Nolie? Are you all right?"

Even as she looked up, Gabe slid into the pew beside her, with Max behind him like a silent shadow.

"Fine." She struggled to smile. "I just felt the need for a little quiet."

Max pushed past Gabe's knees and nuzzled her face, as if he knew her pain.

Gabe's hand closed over hers. "You were praying for my father."

"Yes. Do you know anything new?"

"Not much. It was a heart attack, that's all we know so far."

That was what they'd all been thinking, of course, since they'd heard he'd collapsed.

"Your mother—you should be with her."

He nodded. "I'll go back in a few minutes. I just needed to know you were okay. I didn't expect to find you here." His glance took in the simple, unadorned chapel. "I thought you didn't do organized religion."

"That's what I thought, too."

She could let it go at that. She didn't have to reveal her inner turmoil to him. But she wanted to.

"I saw how much it meant to your mother, having all those people around to support her and pray with her when she needed them. It made me think I might be missing something."

"I'm no expert, that's for sure." His fingers tightened on hers. "You know where I've been lately, spiritually speaking. But I still have to say that I'm grateful for all those other people I know are praying for us."

She'd convinced herself she could be a Christian alone. That she didn't need any company on the journey. Maybe she'd been wrong.

The door behind them swung open, and Brendan popped his head in. "I thought you might be in here."

Gabe surged to his feet. "Any news?"

Brendan's face split in a smile, and a wave of gratitude swept over Nolie. Good news, it had to be, or he wouldn't look that way.

"They've moved your dad to a bed in CCU. He's stabilized, and everything's looking good." He glanced from Gabe to Nolie. "No hurry. They're only letting two people in at a time to see him, anyway."

The door swung shut behind him.

"You should go," she said quickly. "You should be with your mother."

He nodded. "Do you mind sticking around for a while? Just until I see what I'm going to do? She might want me to stay at the house or here at the hospital tonight."

"Of course." She managed a smile. "I'll be glad

to wait, and I can run your things over to the house if need be.''

''Thanks.'' He was frowning, obviously running over in his mind things to be done. Things that didn't include her or the farm.

That was only understandable. He had to be with his family at a time like this. But it began to look as if the few more days she'd thought she had with him were coming to a premature end.

''You can go in now.'' Gabe gave Terry a reassuring smile as he came into hall outside CCU. This had to be especially hard on Terry. She not only knew too much about fire, as he did, she also knew the medical end of it.

She squeezed him quickly and then pushed past him, arranging a smile on her face for Mom and Dad's sake.

Nolie was waiting with Max. Something twisted inside him. Nolie had been here all afternoon, helping everyone. She'd been accepted by the family without question, as if the two of them were a couple.

Nolie was vulnerable. He kept forgetting that, putting his own needs first. But he couldn't do that. He couldn't do anything that would hurt her.

''How are they doing?'' She stroked Max's head, as if the dog gave her comfort.

''Not bad.'' He leaned against the nearest wall, feeling like he'd run a couple miles in full turnout gear. ''When I came out, Mom was scolding Dad for scaring her. And it must have been doing him good, because he was trying to smile.''

Her face relaxed. "That's good to hear. I know how relieved you must be."

He nodded. "Mom—she's amazing. I never understood before just how strong she is. You had a better insight about her than I did."

She shook her head slightly. "I don't know about that. I guess sometimes it's just easier to see things from the outside."

"Maybe so."

Her words touched him. Nolie always seemed to be looking at things from the outside. For the first time he realized how painful that must be. He took her hand, knowing there was no reason to do so, knowing he shouldn't, but wanting to touch her, anyway.

He wanted—well, what did he want? He'd better get this straightened out in his own mind.

He couldn't have it both ways. He and Nolie couldn't both get what they wanted out of this situation, and he was afraid that would always stand between them. Nolie would never be able to forget if his actions cost her the grant. And he'd never be able to forgive if she cost him his job.

It wasn't her fault. It wasn't his. It was just the way things were, and he'd better figure out a way to handle this without anyone getting hurt any more than was inevitable.

"You know, I will take you up on that offer to drop some of my stuff at the house, if you have time. Mom's going to need me for a while."

Something shadowed her eyes, as if she understood what lay behind the words.

"I'd be glad to." She hesitated and then seemed to

make up her mind. "Does this mean you won't be back?"

He tried to keep his face expressionless. "I imagine the chief would excuse me from finishing the training, under the circumstances."

"Of course." She drew her hand away from his carefully. "I guess that's it, then."

He should let her walk away. She wouldn't press him about the foundation, not with his father lying in CCU.

But it wasn't fair. Nolie deserved better than that.

"Look, I don't want it to be this way." She could probably hear the frustration in his voice. "But I can't do what the foundation expects."

"I understand."

She was being a lot more forgiving than he would be, if the situations were reversed.

"I don't want to let you down, Nolie. I'll come back to the farm on Friday for the meeting with the foundation board. I'll try and convince them to give you the funding for your program."

But he wouldn't tell them he needed it. And that could very well be the bottom line.

"Thank you. I appreciate that." Her words were formal. She glanced at Max. "Will you do one other thing for me?"

"Sure." He was too relieved that she was taking it well to argue.

"Keep Max with you for the rest of the week." She lifted her hand to forestall his protest. "I know you think you don't need him, but this is a stressful time. Humor me in this. Please."

"Okay." It was a small enough thing to do for her. "I'll keep him until Friday."

She nodded and patted the dog's head. "Stay, Max." She managed a slight smile. "Please give your parents my best. I'll see you on Friday, then."

For the last time. That was how it had to be.

Chapter Fourteen

Nolie got out of her car at Pastor Brendan's church two nights later, only to discover that her hands were trembling. Clenching her fists, she thrust them into the pockets of her navy blazer.

Obviously those moments in the hospital chapel hadn't been sufficient to wipe out all of her fears. If she'd had a choice, she wouldn't have been going into the church this evening.

But she didn't have a choice. Siobhan Flanagan had called, voice quivering with emotion, and invited her to attend a service of thanksgiving for Joe and Ryan's safety. She hadn't been able to say no.

My fears are irrational, Father. I know that. Please give me the strength to defeat them, once and for all.

She stiffened her spine and walked toward the entrance. She could do this, with God's help.

But maybe it would be safer to claim a seat in one of the back pews. That way, if she had to, she could slip out quietly without disturbing anyone.

Coward, her conscience whispered.

Get through this, she told herself sternly. She had to. Then tomorrow she'd spend working with Danny and two other clients who'd agreed to participate in the demonstration for the foundation on Friday.

And on Friday—well, Friday she'd know her future, one way or another.

It could all come down to what Gabe might say to the foundation board. And she had no control over that at all.

The double doors of the sanctuary stood open, and light poured onto the stream of people who moved inside. Her stomach twisted. She hadn't expected so many people. Well, to be honest, she hadn't known what to expect.

She'd reached the top of the four steps leading into the church when a tall figure stepped toward her. Gabe, with Max at his heels, waited for her.

There was no reason for her heart to thump against her ribs like that. No reason, except that it always seemed to when she saw him, and tonight—

Tonight he wore what must be a dress uniform for firefighters. She'd never seen him in uniform before, of any kind, and the blue jacket with its official insignia changed him, somehow. He seemed even taller, more imposing than he ordinarily did, and that was imposing enough.

As for Max, only the slight waving of his tail indicated that he saw her. Max stood at attention, almost as if he proudly wore a uniform, too.

"We've been waiting for you."

"I hope I'm not late."

Underneath the polite, ordinary words were all the

things she couldn't say. They pressed against her lips and tightened her throat.

Gabe let her precede him into the rear of the sanctuary. Brendan's church, one of the town's oldest ones, had soaring gothic arches that led the eye upward. Tall stained-glass windows lined the sides, and the jewel tones of a rose window above the pulpit glowed from a light behind. It was as far removed as possible from the tiny, barren chapel Brother Joshua had claimed as his.

Gabe extended his arm formally, as if he were escorting her down the aisle at a wedding.

She clasped her hands to keep from reaching out to him. "I thought I'd just slip into one of the back pews."

His gaze seemed to soften in understanding. "My mother wants you to sit with us."

"But—"

I'm not a member of your family, Gabe. I don't belong. After Friday, I'll probably never see you again.

"Please." His voice was low, reaching her under the joyful rush of sound from the organ. "It means so much to her. Don't disappoint her."

That was probably the only thing he could have said that would have persuaded her. She nodded, throat tight, and put her hand on his arm.

He covered it with his other hand, pressing it firmly against his side. A rush of warmth flooded through her, weakening her knees.

Just get through it. She managed a smile and started down the aisle with him.

It was like a wedding, she realized before they were

halfway down the aisle. People were in a mood so joyful that it was contagious, but it was a solemn joy, as if everyone here recognized that something momentous had happened.

There were uniforms throughout the sanctuary, including city police and some others that she didn't recognize. Gabe's words about firefighters going anywhere to honor those who'd died in the line of duty came back to her. They must all be relieved that it wasn't a funeral tonight.

The burgundy carpet seemed to stretch a mile, and she felt as if everyone in the church watched her, wondering who she was and why she was here. Ahead of her, on the communion table, bouquets of spring flowers were massed behind two white candles whose flames flickered and danced.

Finally they reached the front. Siobhan greeted her with a smile and a quick hug, sliding over to make room for them at the end of the pew. Flanagans were crushed into the two front pews, and murmured greetings floated along the row to her.

She sank to the burgundy-cushioned seat, wishing she could slide all the way down to the floor, the way one of Mary Kate's children was trying to do. At least people weren't looking at her any longer.

Then Gabe sat next to her, and her heart turned over once again. They were so crushed in the pew that there was no getting away from him. His hand brushed hers as he reached for a hymnal, and his knee pressed against hers when Max crowded into place on his other side.

Breathe, she told herself, and looked up thankfully

when the organ music ceased and Brendan stepped to the pulpit.

He was in uniform, too. It hadn't occurred to her, but as the fire department chaplain, he would be.

He'd been at the hospital in his role as chaplain, as well as family. In the case of a fatality, the chaplain would be called on, probably, to break the news. How hard that must be for Brendan, given his close ties to the department and its people.

But now, at least, he had a joyful task to perform. He raised his hands, and his smile encompassed the whole congregation.

"Tonight we join the author of Hebrews to declare, 'Let us draw near with confidence to the throne of grace, so that we may receive mercy and find grace to help in time of need.'"

Gabe must have felt her instinctive reaction to the words, because he glanced at her, then wrapped his fingers around hers.

She smiled, hoping he understood that she was all right. No passage Brendan could have chosen would have reassured her more. Those were the words she'd clung to through the darkest times.

Draw near with confidence to the throne of grace.

Brendan couldn't have known that. No one did but God. It was as if He had guided Brendan's thoughts and words. The tension she'd been holding on to since she approached the church seeped away.

The prayers of thanksgiving were still echoing in her heart when Brendan began to pray for the healing of all wounds, visible and invisible. Gabe's fingers tightened painfully around hers.

Her heart contracted. His wounds were invisible,

and so were hers. Brendan's words stirred the air, moving like a breath through the gathered worshippers, as if he were praying directly for them.

The tightness in her heart was suddenly too much to bear. She couldn't carry this any longer. She blinked her eyes against the stinging of tears.

Please, Father. Set me free. I didn't even realize how much I was still held captive by the past, until Gabe entered my life. I don't want to be. I want the freedom You promise.

It was as if the words were a key, releasing all that God wanted to give her. Warmth and lightness flowed through her. It bubbled joyfully through every cell of her body, releasing the bonds that had held her captive for so long.

Her aunt and Brother Joshua had been wrong. She *was* worthy of being loved. How could she have let them deny her that for so long?

Brendan's brief sermon focused on those joyful words from the story of the prodigal son. "Let us celebrate, for this son of mine was dead and is alive again. He was lost, and is found."

Like the son, she'd been lost, but God had found her. She seemed to float through the rest of the service. She felt Gabe's eyes on her several times, as if he sensed a change and wondered at it.

Would she ever have an opportunity to tell him? Probably not, but that didn't seem to matter. No matter how much pain it would cost when Gabe went out of her life, she would still be grateful that knowing him had brought her to this place.

The service ended on a last triumphant hymn, and people flowed toward the doors on a wave of thanksgiving, laughing, talking, and greeting one another. Despite the fact that a number of people stopped Gabe to speak to him, he kept a firm grip on her hand.

She could have pulled free, but she didn't want to. She wanted to believe, even if just for a few minutes, that a bond really did exist between them that could surmount any obstacles in their path.

The line slowed as it reached the outer doors, where Brendan greeted people as they left. He seemed to have a personal word for each one.

Gabe was still talking with the members of a rescue crew from Lancaster, so she occupied herself with glancing over the notices on bulletin board in the vestibule. Brendan clearly had a busy congregation, with everything posted from pleas for donations to a church rummage sale to a workshop for welfare mothers to a youth group car wash.

They reached Brendan then, and he took the hand she extended in both of his. "I'm glad you came tonight, Nolie. Come again, please. You're welcome here."

"Thank you." *Welcome.* The word had a nice sound to it. "I noticed your church is looking for donations to your rummage sale." She squashed a flicker of doubt. "I have a shed full of furniture I can donate, if you have someone with a truck to take it away."

All the while Brendan was assuring her that he'd be glad to do just that, she was aware of the message conveyed by the pressure of Gabe's hand. He understood. He knew what this meant.

She was free of the darkness that had shadowed her life. She had a right to be hopeful for the future.

* * *

"I just hope you don't mess this up."

Gabe looked across the front seat of the car at Terry on Thursday morning. She'd volunteered to drive him to the farm, and apparently she thought that gave her an opportunity to lecture.

"Mess what up?" He might as well be resigned to it. She held him captive for the moment. Nobody had ever kept Terry from saying what she wanted to, in any event.

"Nolie." Terry sent him an exasperated glance. "Don't pretend you don't know what I'm talking about. The woman cares about you, heaven only knows why, and she's one in a million. Don't blow it."

How was it that a sister knew just where a guy was most vulnerable?

"She cares for me the same way she does for all of her clients. In fact, she probably cares more about that lazy donkey she rescued than she does for me."

"Yeah, right. That's why she has stars in her eyes every time she looks at you."

He couldn't help his instant reaction to that. "She does?"

"Please. It's absolutely demoralizing." Terry turned into the farm lane. "The woman's crazy about you. And you can't kid me. You feel the same."

Maybe he couldn't kid her, but she didn't know everything. "It's not as easy as that."

"It never is." Terry pulled to a stop under the willow tree that overhung the lane. "Listen, just take my advice and don't mess it up. You need her."

He slid out, Max at his heels, shutting the door

firmly on anything else she might say. No matter how well-meaning she was, Terry didn't understand what was going on between him and Nolie.

But she was right about one thing. He did need Nolie, just not in the way she thought.

He crossed the lawn toward the training center, trying to find the words that would convince Nolie to do what he wanted. He couldn't seem to find them. Maybe they didn't exist.

The training center was empty except for Lady. She frolicked toward them, and Max looked up as if for permission to play.

"All right, go ahead."

The dogs darted toward the creek, obviously happy to be off duty for a few minutes. He bypassed the paddock and headed into the barn.

Nolie was there. She stood at a stall door, shaking out a bale of straw. Its pale yellow color almost matched the hair she'd pulled into a single long braid down her back.

He stepped forward, his shadow bisecting the oblong of sunlight that lay on the wide, weathered floorboards. She swung toward him, her face expressing surprise at the sight of him and something more—the something more Terry had seen.

She cared for him. And if she cared for him, surely she'd do what he asked.

"Gabe." She brushed her arms free from the cloud of straw. "I didn't expect to see you today. Is everything all right?"

"Fine." He inhaled the mingled aromas of straw, oats and animals, and then shook his head. "Well, maybe not so fine."

She came quickly toward him. "Your father?"

He had to suppress the desire to reach out to her. "No, nothing like that. Dad's doing great."

Her eyes were puzzled. She knew him well enough to know something was wrong.

He may as well come out with it. "I talked to the chief last night after the service." There was no positive light in which to portray what he'd thought. "He's been very supportive with Ryan and Dad. I figured that was a good moment to tackle him about getting back on the job."

"I see." She didn't move, but her face seemed to still.

"It didn't work." He could still hear the chief's voice in his head. "He thinks three injured Flanagans are enough for any department. He offered me a desk job."

"Maybe he's right."

Anger licked at his veins. "No. He's not. I'm not going to sit at a desk for the rest of my working life. I can't."

"You'd still be with the department." The pain in her eyes said she was hurting for him, but she didn't get it.

"I couldn't live like that. I'd rather dig ditches."

"Gabe—" She made a helpless little gesture with her hands. "This doesn't have to be the end of your world. I'm not suggesting ditch-digging, but there's got to be other work you can do that will let you help people."

He shook his head. "I thought you understood how I feel about it."

"I do understand." Passion colored her voice, and she reached toward him.

His fingers tangled with hers, and it was like touching fire. Longing and need surged through him in an engulfing blaze. He pulled her against him, his mouth finding hers with an urgency he'd never felt before. He needed her. He wasn't whole without her.

Nolie melted against him. Her hands moved on his back, drawing him closer, her lips warm and sweet against his. All the problems that rode him seemed to slide away, until nothing was left but Nolie.

He drew his lips from hers reluctantly, trying to get his senses under control. He cradled her face between his palms, his thumbs brushing the pulse that beat in her neck.

"We got off the subject," he said softly. "My fault."

"No. Mine." She murmured the words, tears still shimmering in her eyes. "Gabe, I wish so much that I could do something to make this right for you."

He took a breath, trying to clear his head. Nolie wanted to help—that was the important thing. She knew how much this meant to him.

"You can do something."

Frown lines formed between her brows. "I don't understand. You said the chief—"

"I asked the chief what it would take to convince him to put me back on active duty. He said he'd need a strong statement from an unbiased source to back up his decision." He rushed on, needing to get the words out. "An unbiased professional source, Nolie. Like you."

The Lang woman has seen you in action for the past

*month. Get her to declare in writing that you're ready
for action, and I'll take a chance.*

It had come down to this. Nolie held his future in
the palms of her hands. If she cared about him, she'd
do the right thing.

The realization of what Gabe was asking her sank
into Nolie's heart like lead. He wanted her to lie for
him.

Please, Gabe. Don't make me say no to you. Please.

She caught her breath, trying to marshal the arguments that would make him see what he was doing.

"Gabe, you must know that won't do any good.
Why would he be impressed by anything I might
say?"

"He knows how much we've been working together. He trusts your judgment."

I don't. Not where you're concerned.

"I'm not a medical professional. You should get the
doctor to talk to him."

"No." His mouth clamped shut on the word.

"You haven't told the doctor about your seizure,
have you?" Her heart sank. This was worse than she'd
thought.

"Look, there was no point in telling the doctor
about it. He'd just have given me a lecture about staying on the meds, and I didn't need that." His mouth
twisted. "I'd already found that out for myself."

"But—" Her mind whirled with all the ways his
reasoning was flawed. "Will they let you back on active duty when you're on the medication?"

"I don't know." His uncompromising tone made it
clear he didn't intend to find out.

"You didn't tell the chief about the medication." She tried to swallow her disappointment. "Gabe, the department has to know. It shouldn't make a difference, but you have to tell them."

He shook his head, the set of his jaw stubborn. "It will just bring up an issue that's better avoided. I'll probably never have another seizure, and I'll be able to get off the medication eventually with no one the wiser."

"You can't be sure of that."

"You said yourself that last seizure was a mild one. They're tapering off."

"I hope that's true." Desperation made her words sharp. "But I don't know that, and neither do you. You've got to give yourself more time."

"I don't have time. Dad may never get back to work, and someone has to keep an eye on Ryan."

"After the scare he had with your father, Ryan will surely take more care."

He was already shaking his head. "Ryan won't change. He was born that way—too much charm and too much luck. It makes him take chances."

"Seth and Terry are still there to look out for him. Why does it have to be you?"

"He doesn't listen to them. I'm the oldest son. I'm responsible for the others. You don't know what it's like."

That stung, but she kept her gaze steady on his. "No. I never had family to care for."

"I'm sorry." Regret filled his eyes. "I shouldn't have said that."

"It's true. I don't understand that kind of family responsibility. But I know you're taking just as much risk as Ryan ever does if you try to go back on active duty now.''

''I won't have a seizure on the job.''

A chill seemed to settle deep into her soul. ''If you were sure of that, you'd be talking to the doctor, not to me.''

His face hardened. ''I can't take that chance, Nolie. You're the only one who can help me.''

''Please.'' Her voice shook, and all the will in the world wouldn't keep it steady. ''Don't ask me.''

''I have to.'' He caught her wrists in his hands. His pain seemed to pass through that touch straight to her heart. ''If you love me, you'll do this for me.''

Pain twisted her very soul. She had to say the words, even knowing they'd put an end to everything between them.

''I do love you. But I can't let you put yourself and other people in danger. I can't do it.''

He dropped her hands, and her pulse beat against the empty air. Gabe turned and stalked out of the barn.

Chapter Fifteen

"**Y**ou're going where?" Gabe frowned at his mother.

"You heard me. We're going to Nolie's. The least she deserves from the Flanagan family is a bit of support when she confronts the foundation board." She gave him what the Flanagan siblings generally referred to as *the look*. "You should be there as well, Gabriel."

Terry and his father stood waiting by the door, their expressions indicating that they were fresh out of sympathy for him.

"I can't." He clamped his mouth shut on the word. He wasn't about to start explaining himself to every member of his family. "But if you're going, you may as well take Max back to Nolie."

Max looked up from his spot on the living-room rug at the sound of his name, his tail waving gently.

"I'm afraid you'll have to do that yourself." His usually gentle mother seemed to have undergone a transformation since Dad had come home from the hospital. "That's your responsibility, not ours."

She marched out with Dad and Terry following, the snap of the door reflecting her annoyance with him.

He frowned at Max. He never should have brought the dog home with him from the farm the day before, but by the time he'd realized that Terry had put Max in the car, he hadn't wanted to go back to the barn for an anticlimactic conversation with Nolie about him.

"Sorry, boy. Nothing personal. But Nolie might as well give you to someone who needs you."

The dog's tail waved again at the sound of Nolie's name. Looked as if both of them were stuck with a reaction to that sound. How long would it take him to get over that?

Maybe never.

He rubbed the throbbing that had been going on in his temples since he'd walked out on Nolie the day before. Why did she have to make this so hard? She could just have agreed to do what he wanted.

No, she couldn't. She's not that kind of a person. You should have known that before you asked it of her.

His conscience seemed to speak in time with the pounding in his head. Maybe another hour of sleep would help.

"I'm going upstairs to lie down, Max. You stay."

Before he'd reached the steps the dog was there. Max put that big yellow body of his across the bottom of the staircase and barked at him.

"What's the matter with you?" The dog was about as stubborn as Nolie was. "Get out of the way."

Max whined, obviously distressed. He took a step or two away from the stairs, but instead of letting Gabe start up, he shoved him toward the center of the rug.

"Get away, Max." His head was spinning so badly he could barely focus on the dog. "Leave me alone."

Max barked again, sharply, and then put his shoulder against Gabe's legs, pushing him away from the lamp table.

Gabe stumbled. Felt himself losing control. Saw the carpet coming up to meet him as blackness poured over him in a sickening wave.

His last conscious thought was that Max had done just what Nolie hoped he would—he'd sensed the seizure coming on and warned him.

He didn't have any idea how long it was until he came to awareness again—maybe seconds, maybe an hour. The warm, strong body of the dog was curved protectively against him and the cushioned carpet cradled his body. Max was responsible. The dog had made certain he didn't hurt himself when he fell.

Max whined. Then, as if he knew the worst was over, he licked Gabe's face.

The worst was over. He repeated the words in his mind as he struggled to overcome the lassitude that seemed to settle into his bones. He put his arms around Max, leaning on his strength.

He couldn't ignore this seizure. It had been worse than the last, not slighter. And he'd been taking the meds regularly.

I can't let you put yourself and other people in danger.

Nolie's voice rattled in his head, bringing with it a

vivid image of just how bad it would be to have a seizure when he was on the job.

Anger swept through him like a flame caught by the wind. *Why, God? Why did You let this happen to me? How could You do this to me? Haven't I always tried to do what You wanted? Why are You taking away the thing I want most in the world? It's not fair.*

Max whined, as if sensing his anger and not knowing what to do with it. He turned his face into Max's fur. He couldn't pretend any longer.

His life as a firefighter was over, at least for now. Maybe forever. Tears stung his eyes and soaked into the dog's coat as he grieved for the life that he'd lost.

When, finally, he was still, he seemed to hear again the Voice that whispered in his heart.

There are other things for you to do. Good things. Your life isn't over. It's just beginning.

Nolie had said she'd taken the first step toward healing when she'd let herself be angry with God. It looked as if she'd been right. He couldn't be spiritually whole until he'd let out the anger he'd been hiding deep inside.

Nolie. He could almost see the love in her eyes. Nolie had overcome far worse things than this, and she'd gone on to do good work. She deserved a chance to do even more, and he was letting her down.

"This is no time to be unable to drive," he told Max as he fumbled in his pocket for his cell phone. "We have to get to Nolie."

He had to. Whether there could be anything between them he didn't know, but he had to help her. If standing up in front of his family and the foundation board and admitting his disability would do that, that's what he'd do. If he could get there in time.

"Please," he murmured, just as Brendan answered the phone.

"Are you sure you understand what I want you and Lady to do?"

Nolie looked down at Danny with concern. The boy seemed unusually nervous about this. Maybe she shouldn't have asked it of him, but without Gabe to talk to the foundation board, what else could she do? Someone had to demonstrate the value of her work.

"I guess so." Danny ruffled Lady's fur, and the dog pressed closer to the wheelchair as if she felt his tension. "I just wish Gabe was here."

The knife in her heart twisted a little. Maybe someday she would get used to the pain.

"I know," she said softly. "I wish that, too."

"Why isn't he?" Danny focused on her face, his eyes wide and a little frightened. "Doesn't he like us anymore?"

Me, not you. It's me he doesn't like.

"Of course he likes us." She put her arms around Danny for a quick hug. "It's just—well, it's like we talked about once. Grown-ups sometimes don't act in a very grown-up way when they care a lot about something. Gabe has some problems he has to work out."

Or not. She'd done everything she could to reach him, and she'd failed.

They'd talked about that the day Gabe had rescued her from Danny's father. She'd never forget the look on Gabe's face that day. He'd cared about her—she knew it.

He just hadn't cared enough.

"I hope he works them out soon. I want to see him." Danny's words were an echo of what was in her heart.

She couldn't let herself obsess about Gabe now. She'd have plenty of time later to mourn what they might have been to each other. For now, she had to concentrate on the next task.

She bent to bring her face close to Danny's. "You're going to do fine, Danny. You and Lady are great together."

He nodded, a look of determination on his thin face. "We'll do it. We won't let you down."

"That's my hero." She hugged him again.

Danny patted her shoulder, as if he were the adult and she were the child. "Gabe'll come back. I know he will."

"I hope so. Either way, we're going to be fine."

Her throat was tight, but Danny's courage seemed to clear her mind. She glanced across the training center to see Siobhan, Terry and Joe sitting in the folding chairs behind the foundation board. But not Gabe.

She'd done all she could. She'd tried her best to be faithful. All she could do now was trust that God would work this situation out for the best.

Please, Father...

She looked up again and saw Gabe and Max walk slowly through the door.

Her heart began thudding against her ribs. She waited for him to join his family. Instead he crossed the floor toward her and Danny.

She tried to analyze his expression. He had shadows under his eyes that she hadn't seen before. But he also looked as if he'd come to a conclusion that had brought him peace.

Maybe he'd come up with some other way to convince the chief to let him back on the job. She couldn't think of anything else that would put that look in his eyes.

"Hi, Gabe." Danny's face was suffused with joy. "I knew you'd come. I told Nolie so."

Gabe ruffled his hair. "I couldn't miss this. How are you doing, buddy?"

"Scared," Danny said. "I didn't want to do this all by myself."

Gabe's eyes met hers, and her pulse rate shot up. "How about you?"

"Scared, too." She clenched and unclenched her hands. "I didn't expect to see you today."

"I'm here." He put his hand on Danny's shoulder. "I couldn't let my buddy do this all by himself."

"That's good." She managed a smile. That was it, then. He'd come out of loyalty to Danny.

Well, what else could she expect? He'd try to convince the board her program was worthwhile. That was all she could hope for.

"Ms. Lang?" Mr. Henley's voice echoed across the room. "Are we about ready to start?"

"Right away," she called back.

She divided her smile between man and boy. "I'll be right over by the board members, explaining to them everything you're doing. You'll be great."

She hoped. *Please, Father. It's in Your hands now.*

One way or another, he would get the grant for Nolie. Her work was too important to let this slip away. As for whatever else might happen between them—

Well, that would have to wait until this was settled.

Nolie was already telling the group what they were about to see. He put his hand on Danny's shoulder.

"Okay?"

"I'm a little bit scared about the gate." Danny looked down at the hands that wouldn't always do what he wanted.

"Try to pretend no one else is here. Just you and Lady, me and Max. It'll be like the day you and Lady showed us how to do it. Remember that?"

A faint smile showed. "I remember. I missed you when you weren't here."

It was like a punch to the heart. Hurting Nolie had been bad, and hurting a child was even worse, if possible.

"I've been a jerk lately, Danny. I'm sorry."

"It's okay. I told Nolie you wouldn't let us down."

His heart eased a bit. "You did, did you? What did Nolie say to that?"

Danny's face relaxed in a grin. "She said sometimes grown-ups don't act very grown up."

Maybe that meant she'd forgive him. "I'm not sure I'm grown up yet, but I will try."

"Like my dad." Danny nodded toward the audience. "Did you see? He's here. I want to do a good job so he'll be proud of me."

"You know what? My dad's here, too." And he had similar feelings to Danny's. How would his father take the news that Gabe would no longer be a firefighter?

He wasn't going to express any doubt to Danny. "I happen to think they'll both be proud of us, even if we make a mistake."

Nolie was introducing them. His stomach felt about the way it had when he'd run on the field for his first Little League game.

"Here we go," he whispered. "Remember, I'll be right behind you."

Be behind both of us, Father.

They moved toward the first obstacle, with Nolie explaining the differences in how the dogs worked with each of them. He kept his eyes fixed on Danny, a prayer forming in his heart, knowing that Nolie was probably praying the same prayer now, too.

He began to relax as they went through the familiar routine. Both dogs, seeming to know they had an audience, performed flawlessly.

Finally Danny and Lady approached the gate, the final obstacle. He held his breath.

You can do it, Danny. I know you can.

The boy reached for the latch, struggling to make his fingers work. He almost had it. Lady, sensing his tension, pushed too soon, and the latch snapped shut.

Danny's small face tightened, as if he held back tears, and Gabe's heart ached for him.

"Easy," he said softly. His fingers twitched with the longing to do it for him, but that wouldn't help Danny. "Slow and steady, remember?"

The boy bit his lip and nodded. Again he reached for the latch. Slowly, agonizingly slowly, he pushed it to the open position. Instantly Lady's shoulder was against the gate, opening it.

Danny turned toward him, grinning, and gave him the thumbs-up sign as the audience, including the foundation board, burst into applause.

Heart overflowing with pride and thanksgiving,

Gabe returned the signal. He looked at Nolie. Her eyes were bright with tears, and her smile trembled.

He knew what she was thinking. Was this going to be enough to convince them? There was one more obstacle he had to face, and it was the hardest one.

Crossing the space between them, he joined Nolie. "If it's all right with you, I'd like to address the board."

She nodded.

He moved toward the table, taking a moment to glance at the people in the rows of chairs behind the foundation board. Danny's parents, the families of several other of Nolie's clients. The chief. Dad, Mom, Terry. Seth, in uniform, must have come straight from the station, and he stood next to Ryan. The Flanagans were out in force. Even Brendan, who'd driven him here, sat next to Nolie's friend, Claire.

The sight distracted him for a moment. Brendan had better be careful. That woman would have him for lunch.

He wouldn't have chosen this public spot to tell the people in his life, but this was how it had worked out. He looked at Nolie, and his jittery nerves stilled.

This was for Nolie.

Nolie clasped her hands in front of her, then realized how tense that must look and dropped them to her sides. There was probably no hope for that—her nervousness must be apparent to anyone who looked at her. Her future could be riding on what Gabe said to the board.

If Gabe told them he didn't need Max, it could sway

them away from funding her no matter what else he said.

Please, Father, she began, and then remembered her earlier prayer. *I put it in Your hands.*

Once again the tension slid away, and she was able to listen to Gabe without fearing the results.

"You've heard all about the program Ms. Lang runs here." He seemed relaxed, one hand resting lightly on Max's head. "There's probably very little additional information I can give you. However, I would like to speak about my personal experience with Nolie's Ark."

The board members watched him intently. Probably all of them knew that Samuel Henley had been instrumental in putting Gabe into the program as a test case.

"I would like to say, first, that this program deserves your support regardless of whether my training with the seizure alert dog was successful. You've seen some of her amazing results for yourselves."

A few head nods among the board members, but Nolie's heart sank. How impressed would they be if Gabe declared he didn't need the dog?

You could tell them about his seizure, a voice whispered temptingly in her mind. You could say he's not being fair to the program.

No, she couldn't. No matter what happened, she wouldn't do that to him.

"But the fact is that the training I've had here has been successful."

Gabe glanced toward her, and she could only stare back at him.

"As some of you may know, I received an injury on the job that caused me to have seizures." His voice seemed to deepen on the words that couldn't be easy for him to speak. "I had hoped that the condition was only temporary, and frankly, I fought participating in the program at all."

His gaze seemed to sweep the audience then, and she knew he was watching his parents' reaction.

"But this morning I had another seizure, a bad one. And I want to tell you that the dog Ms. Lang trained for me performed beyond anything I could have imagined."

Her heart clenched painfully, hurting for him. Another seizure. Gabe must have been devastated.

"Max knew the seizure was coming before I did. He kept me from starting up the stairs, knowing that I could have been seriously injured if the seizure had hit there." He smiled down at the dog. "He pushed me into a safe location in spite of my objections. If it hadn't been for Max, I'm not sure what might have happened."

Her throat was so tight she couldn't have spoken if she'd had to. But she didn't have to. Gabe was saying it all.

"So you see, I'm a textbook example of what Ms. Lang's program can do. She helps so many people, and she deserves the chance to help many more. Please, be sure that Nolie's Ark can continue its work. A lot of people with disabilities, like Danny and me, are counting on you."

Applause swept the room as he finished. Danny gave him a thumbs-up sign.

The tears she'd been trying to hold back spilled

over, and she put her hands to her face to wipe them away, smiling.

She didn't know whether the foundation board would agree with Gabe or not, but either way, she had won.

Chapter Sixteen

❧

"Thank you." Nolie responded to one more congratulatory hug, this time from Siobhan Flanagan. "And thank you for bringing all this food."

She gestured toward her dining-room table, which had been turned into an impromptu buffet for all the food the Flanagans had brought. The announcement that the foundation board was going to fund her program completely had apparently, to the Flanagans, seemed like a good reason for a party.

"It's nothing."

Siobhan grabbed one of her grandchildren as he toddled by, swinging the little boy up in her arms for a hug. Mary Kate had arrived soon after the announcement, with her children and Seth's little boy, loaded with even more food.

"It seems like something to me. I've never had a party here before."

Once she said the words, she saw how strange that

was. She'd let her memories affect her more than she'd realized.

She smiled. Any dark fragments from her aunt's era were surely wiped clean of the house by the sounds of this celebration.

"Well, you deserve more than a party. I can't thank you enough for what you've done for Gabriel." Siobhan's eyes glistened with tears.

Nolie watched as Joe Flanagan bent Samuel Henley's ear about something. "Is Gabe's father all right with this?"

"You know, I think he is." Siobhan smiled fondly across the room at her husband. "Maybe his brush with his own mortality opened his eyes just a bit. He's starting to see that there are other good things in life besides fire fighting."

"I'm glad. It would hurt Gabe to feel he was letting his father down."

"Gabe's a grown man now." Siobhan patted her arm. "It's time he looked for approval to someone other than his father."

She didn't know what to say. Siobhan was looking at her as if she were that someone, and—

"Is this a private conversation, or can anyone join in?"

The sound of Gabe's voice set her heart beating faster, and she turned to find him smiling at her.

"You can talk to Nolie," his mother declared, hoisting the toddler in her arms. "I'm going to find something to feed this child." She moved off toward the buffet table.

"I can't believe your family did all this." She tried to keep her voice normal as she gestured to the overflowing room. "I'd never even thought of having a party, and they put it together in ten minutes flat."

"If there's one thing Flanagans know how to do, it's eat. And interfere."

She managed to smile as she met his gaze. "I'm happy for this sort of interference."

"You won't be so happy when they start telling you how to live your life," he said darkly, but the corner of his mouth twitched.

"I owe them. And you. Especially you."

Tears stung her eyes, and she blinked them back. There was no reason to cry, and she'd embarrass Gabe if she did.

"You don't owe me a thing, except maybe a quiet place to talk." He grasped her arm and steered her to the door. "Let's get out of here for a minute."

But when they reached the porch, they found Brendan and Claire sitting on the swing. Nolie blinked. What an unlikely pair that was. Did Claire realize Brendan was a minister?

"See, that's what happens when you get involved with Flanagans." Gabe glared at his cousin. "There's too darned many of them."

Brendan just smiled. "A couple of the kids are in the training center playing with the dogs, but I think the barn's unoccupied at the moment."

"Fine." Holding her hand firmly, Gabe tugged her behind him as he strode toward the barn.

"Gabe, wait a minute." She tried without success to pull her hand away. "I can't walk out on the party."

"They'll never even notice we're missing, and I don't care if they do." He slowed as they reached the barn door and looked at her with an intensity that seared. "I have something to say to you. I'll do it in front of the family if I have to, but I'd rather do it in private."

Her heart seemed to be beating somewhere up in her throat, and she didn't trust her voice to say a word. She nodded and let him propel her into the barn.

Gabe's forward momentum stopped at the first stall, and she caught her breath. They'd kissed here, once. Was he thinking of that?

"What—what did you want to say?"

"First, thank you." His frown cut off any objection she might make. "Not just about the dog, although he saved me from a serious fall today. Thank you for refusing to do what I asked you to."

"I didn't want to refuse. I had to."

"I know." He held both of her hands in his, and he looked down at their clasped fingers for a moment, as if trying to decide what to say. "You were right. What if that seizure today had happened when I was on duty, with lives depending on me?" A shudder went through him, so painful she could feel it. "I can't believe I was willing to risk that."

"You didn't realize. It's hard to accept that the life you want is out of your reach."

Even as she said the words, Nolie knew that they applied to her, too. There was a life she wanted now, one she hadn't been able to dream about before. But whether or not she got that life depended on Gabe.

"My days as an active firefighter are gone, at least for now." His grip tightened. "Maybe, someday, I'll be well enough to go back, but it won't be until I'm sure. Until then, I guess I need Max after all."

Just Max.

"Max is yours. You and he both know that." She wouldn't let him see that she was hurting. "What are you going to do now?"

"I talked to the chief again. We both know a desk job isn't for me, but he offered me a training spot instead. He seems to think I might do a good job of teaching what I know about fire fighting."

"That's good, isn't it?" She looked at him anxiously. "At least you'll still be involved with the department."

He nodded. "It's only part-time, though. I was thinking that with the grant and expanding your program, maybe you could use some help around here. What do you think?"

"I—"

She struggled to find an answer. How could she stand to work with him every day if a business relationship was all he wanted?

"Or there's an alternative plan." His fingers moved on hers. "If you don't like the idea of a business partner, maybe you'd settle for a life partner."

Her gaze leaped to his face, and her heart pounded against her ribs. "A life partner?" She whispered the words.

"You're already an honorary Flanagan. How about making it the real thing?" He lifted her hands, and she felt the warm touch of his lips against her fingers.

"Nolie, I've seen my world turn upside down lately, but I've learned some things in the process. Love isn't about being strong or weak. It's about caring for each other and depending on each other."

"Yes." Her thoughts flitted to Joe and Siobhan.

"I know that I love you." Gabe's voice was as

solemn as if they stood in church. "For keeps. Will you marry me?"

If the song in her heart got any louder, he'd hear it. Nolie felt the last dark remnants of the past falling away as she raised her face to his.

"Yes. Oh, yes."

His arms went around her, drawing her close. They stood there, not kissing, just holding each other. She felt the steady beating of his heart against her cheek. From beyond the barn door came the sound of laughter and children's voices, then the braying of the donkey.

Thank You, Father. Thank You.

Her heart filled with joy. God had given her more than she'd ever dreamed possible. She and Gabe would be together forever, and Nolie's Ark was going to overflow with their happiness.

* * * * *

Dear Reader,

I'm so glad you decided to pick up this book, and I hope my story touched your heart. Helping Nolie and Gabe surmount the obstacles that separated them was a wonderful writing experience for me.

It was also exciting to learn more about the wonderful work done by service animals and those devoted individuals who train them, and to remind myself again of the heroism and self-sacrifice of firefighters.

I hope you'll write and let me know how you liked this story. Address your letter to me at Steeple Hill Books, 233 Broadway, New York, NY 10279, and I'll be happy to send you a signed bookplate or bookmark. You can visit me on the Web at www.martaperry.com or e-mail me at marta@martaperry.com.

Blessings,

Marta Perry

HEART AND SOUL

BY

JILLIAN HART

Taking in an injured stranger wasn't something
Michelle McKaslin would normally do, but she'd
sensed something special about Gabe Brody. But
would her heaven-sent feelings remain when she
learned who he really was—the undercover agent
investigating her family?

Don't miss

HEART AND SOUL
On sale May 2004.

Available at your favorite retail outlet.

Visit Steeple Hill Books online and...

EXPLORE new titles in Online Reads—new romances every month available only online!

LEARN more about the authors behind your favorite Steeple Hill and Love Inspired titles—read interviews and more on the Authors' page.

JOIN our lively discussion groups. Topics include prayer groups, recipes and writers' sessions. You can find them all on the Discussion page.

In today's turbulent world, quality inspirational fiction is especially welcome, and you can rely on Steeple Hill to deliver it in every book.

Steeple
Hill®

HEARTS IN BLOOM

BY

MAE NUNN

Landscape designer Jessica Holliday needed to make a name for herself, and a society wedding was just the place to do it. But someone didn't want Jessica to succeed…. Enter Andrew Keegan, who thought God's plan meant marriage to a socialite in order to help others. Would Drew see his goal change—with Jessica as his new bride-to-be?

Don't miss

HEARTS IN BLOOM
On sale May 2004.

Available at your favorite retail outlet.

LOVE KNOT

BY

SUSAN KIRBY

Mending their broken marriage was not something Paula Blake Jackson wanted. But she would do anything for her beloved child, even reconcile with the man who'd abandoned her when she'd needed him most. Yet Colton had been hurt by the pain of the past, too. Would the daughter he'd never known give Colton the chance to win back his family?

Don't miss

LOVE KNOT

On sale May 2004.

Available at your favorite retail outlet.